Had she ~~~~~~~~~~~~~~ cougar's lair?

The light changed, as if a shadow passed by. Ann's breath froze. "Is someone else here?"

Above, loft boards creaked. Dust sprinkled into the shafts of light around her. Her mind raced as a rapid pounding claimed her heart. *Don't panic.* She forced a breath against the tightening of her chest.

Frantic eyes searched for an exit. The stall door held her only escape. Ann took shallow breaths as she moved toward the other side of the room. The dirt floor softened her footsteps. Once there, she paused and twirled her hair.

The open front of the barn stood partially visible. Ann strained to see or hear something . . . anything outside the opening. She started forward.

Thump.

A startled shriek escaped her lips.

Had something heavy fallen from the loft?

She held her breath. A crash followed a blur of movement. Something large made a quick retreat.

Ann screamed.

Coming Sequels by Regina Tittel

Unexpected Kiss

Coveted Bride

Cherished Stranger

Abandoned Hearts

Regina Tittel

♡♡♡

ABANDONED HEARTS

Published by Hawespipe Ministries
Copyright © 2011 by Regina Tittel
Cover design by Regina Tittel

All Scripture quotations are taken from the King James Version.

ISBN-13: 978-1463620271
ISBN-10: 1463620276

Regina Tittel's books are written to uplift and encourage each individual while also entertaining them with a great story. It is the author's prayer that Abandoned Hearts will clearly explain the benefit of scripture memorization and abstinence before marriage. Just because one dedicates their life to Christ doesn't mean they'll no longer be tempted. Temptations are the same for everyone; it is how we prepare ourselves for them that make the difference.

For whatsoever things were written aforetime, were written for our learning, that through patience and comfort of the scriptures we might have hope.

—Romans 15:4

Tremendous thanks go to so many encouraging people that made this possible. I'd like to thank my Savior, Jesus Christ, who gifted me with the passion and ability to write.

Thank you to my personal hero and inspiration for every hero I pen, my husband, Jerad. Your faith in me is overwhelming and your steadfast love makes our story a true fairytale.

Our two beautiful children have been wonderfully supportive which only made this more possible. Thank you, girls, I love you so much.

Thank you, also, to those that cheered me on, even in the beginning stages and endured my earliest versions of this story, my mom and dad, Janet, Dorena, Krista, Harold, Ginny, Shea, Diana, Fay, Kay, Patty, Laura, Emily, Julie, and Ashlee.

Also, thanks to my wonderful critique partners, Mildred, Rebecca, and everyone else at Scribes 216 and Scribes 218. I would not be here without you!

Chapter One

Ann McHaven slumped against the torn seat of the truck. The jagged vinyl she'd earlier avoided leaning against, now jabbed her back. She despised being stuck in the middle of the dirt road, though the comparison to her life was almost laughable. Her eyes darted in both directions, not a car in sight. No need to coax the truck to the side. The road looked abandoned.

She forced the heavy door to open against the cool March wind and stepped down. Hiking boots cushioned her feet from the course gravel. Her worried gaze took in the remote environment as she twirled a strand of hair.

Cattle grazed scattered about in dry fields, content to munch away on large bales of hay. Along the fence line bordering the road, trees boasted tiny buds perched on the ends of their branches. Each promised a change to the bleak winter landscape.

Ann released a sigh and turned back to the truck.

A forward thrust of the bench-seat revealed a jack. Dirt coated it in a gritty layer along with the unwelcome smell of grease. *Yuck*. She picked up a red, shop towel to protect her hands. *Though, it's better than the smell of alcohol and sweat.* She fought against the memory and knelt down on her hands and knees to slide the jack underneath the truck, grimacing as rocks dug into her delicate skin.

It's a good thing Uncle Frank taught me how to use this thing, 'cause I'd turn gray waiting for a rescue all the way out here. Like a child recovering a toy from underneath a couch, she lowered her shoulders to the ground to peer under the truck.

"Okay, Ann, don't put it under the sway bar, just a solid part of the frame," she mumbled. Her neck tingled as her nerves grew more agitated. Being helpless and apart from any family to depend on wasn't something she wanted to repeat.

Mental images pushed past her feeble attempt to block them.

Positioned at the end of the hall, her room had been her safe-haven. Since she was the hired nanny no one ever entered, until that night. Why? She had never led him on. Or had she? Guilt churned her stomach. Her throat clogged with emotion. Had she been guilty, or was she simply reacting from the gossip they'd spread? Her employers' art of twisting the truth was astounding. Doubt now clouded her self-assurance.

She needed someone to talk to. Who could she tell, who would understand that after two months she still couldn't move on?

Ann refocused on the job at hand. "God, please help me find the right spot, and please keep me safe . . ." She blew a stray hair out of her eyes. "Oh, who cares?"

Heaven sounded better all the time.

While Ann looked over her options, the stir of gravel interrupted her thoughts. A voice laced with a condescending tone followed.

"It seems to me with darkness closing in, any female in her right mind would ask for safety. Especially with the type of wild critters we have." The man's deep voice held the same Midwestern accent as her uncle's. "But I guess our minds don't think much alike."

Ann raised her head and thumped it on the truck. Pain shot through her skull. *Arrggg.* She rubbed the forming knot and resisted the urge to look behind her. *Don't expose any sign of fear.* Experience taught her weirdo's loved defenseless women.

She continued with the jack as though unperturbed. "I guess you proved your last statement right, because it would seem to me that any kind of *gentleman*, would want to help out a lady in distress. Or, do they not have those here in the Ozarks?"

A half laugh escaped the man's throat. Ann noticed the sound came from an unusual height and turned her head.

Curiosity had always been her weakness.

Hooves? Her eyes followed up the horse's legs to its rider. Broad shoulders and a slightly barreled chest evoked authority, while his powerful limbs appeared to possess the muscular strength of someone accustomed to hard labor. His entire essence demanded respect. As he shifted in the saddle, he blocked the glare of the setting sun.

Dark brows were knitted in a serious fashion over twinkling blue eyes, and a straight nose led to hardened lips. Ann was certain he was trying to resist the urge to laugh at her. Again.

She must have stared too long, because her knight on pale steed broke the silence.

"What business do you have out here anyway?"

His words came across arrogant. Added to his condescending humor, Ann found him unlikable.

But handsome.

Don't do anything to lead him on.

As she stood, dirt fell from her clothes like rain. She dusted off her faded jeans and flannel shirt careful not to inhale the chalky air. With her chin lifted, she flipped her low ponytail over one shoulder. To add to her appearance of confidence, she stood with her feet apart and her arms crossed in front. "I have just as much right to this road as any other. And as for my business, that's exactly what it is. Mine."

With a roll of his shoulder and a slight sigh, the man shook his head and dismounted.

The muscles in her lower back tensed. Unconscious of her actions, she inched against the truck.

The stranger dropped the leather reins, and with two strides came within a foot of Ann. He smelled like a mixture of pine, hay . . . and horse. His gaze dropped to her lips. Her whole body stiffened. She fought the urge to squirm and tunneled her nervous energy into words.

"Are you going to change my tire for me or just tell me how to do it?"

He raised an eyebrow. "Maybe I had something different in mind."

Though her skin hadn't prickled with alarm, she wasn't about to leave things to chance. She raised the handle of the jack. "I don't respond well to threats, Mister."

He dropped his sarcasm and softened his voice. "I was referring to giving you a ride home." His eyes still revealed humor, but at least he controlled his smirk.

The handle dropped to her side, while Ann studied him. "I don't accept rides from strangers."

With a single hand, he reached over her shoulder and grabbed the spare. He sat it down and examined it with a scowl. "This won't get you any further than that one. It's nearly flat and past dry-rotted."

Like I wouldn't have noticed that. Besides, how does he think he'll get me home? On a horse? She fought to silence her uncommon, smart-aleck attitude.

"Well if you're not going to change it, please step aside, because I am. I don't have far to go, and I'm sure it'll do." She reached to roll the tire from his hands.

The man brushed her hands away. "Humph. You are a stubborn one, aren't you?"

A jolt surged through her. Before she could give it consideration he spoke again. "How 'bout I change it, then this *stranger*, who prefers to be known as *Jacob*, will plan on picking you up in an hour? I'm sure by then you'll be tired of walkin'." He didn't wait for a response and proceeded to change her tire.

"Life's insulted me enough. I don't need you adding to it." Ann's throat tightened. Her attention dropped to the road as she scuffed the gravel with the toe of her shoe. Life sure turned out different than she dreamed it would. If it weren't for her drunken employer, she'd still have a job. And if it weren't for his actions, she wouldn't feel so uncomfortable around men.

Though, despite her misunderstanding of his offer, this stranger didn't alarm her. The familiar feeling of fear had yet to course its way up her spine.

While her bewildering rescuer worked in silence, Ann took a closer look. No wedding band on his left hand. Why had she even thought to look there? It's not as if she liked being near him, let alone entertained the thought of something more. He was too confident and cocky, which made her defensive.

Probably a reflex, she reasoned, given her recent encounters with married men. Maybe a worthy distraction *was* what she needed in life. But her distraction would have to be the opposite of—what did he say his name was—Jacob?

Her eyes trailed back. His boots were of worn leather, the heels needed replaced and his jeans were of no significant brand. A far cry from the men she used to be around.

His lined, denim shirt's top two buttons were undone, revealing a chest full of hair. Not your smooth-skinned poster boy, but definitely real male. She smiled as her gaze drew up to his thick wavy crown of hair. Before she allowed herself to imagine what it would feel like between her fingers, she adjusted her attention to the setting sun.

Jacob tightened the last lug nut and glanced up. He rose to his feet and seemed like a beacon of strength to her small frame. His voice broke the stillness of the cool evening. "What's your name?" He brushed his hands against his thighs.

His very muscular thighs.

"Ann." The answer slipped from her mouth before she could stop it. She bit the inside of her lip out of pure frustration. His movements distracted her. Why couldn't he stand still?

"Well, *Ann*, do you have any idea what the road is like up ahead?"

Pretty, peaceful, with an even exchange of field and forest? Of course, she didn't know what it was like. She'd never driven on this country road before. But to allow him that knowledge would give away her vulnerability. That would be the last thing she did.

Ann tightened her jaw and said nothing.

He sighed, seeming exasperated. "It meets a wide stream. Once you cross it, you can only go so far on the gravel, before it meets back up with water. Only this time, you don't cross the creek. The road turns *into* the creek. And if you're not experienced with this truck's four-wheel drive, you'll never make it through."

She remained silent.

Jacob's eyes narrowed. "Do you understand? You'll have to maneuver through the creek bed for a while before the road becomes a road again."

"I know what I'm doing." *Liar.* A little voice inside niggled at her conscience.

Jacob shook his head. "Hopefully that tire will get you back before the sun goes down." He reached out and flipped the end of her collar. "'Cause I imagine that thin flannel's not going to keep you warm if you have to walk."

Ann's chin dropped as she glanced at her shirt, but quickly lifted again. *How dare he touch my shirt?* She squared her shoulders and let her mulish attitude take full control. "Thanks. I have no doubt I'll make it."

Jacob shook his head. Had she convinced him? Probably not. It was a valiant effort of pride, the result of a hard head.

He effortlessly tossed the ruined tire into the back of the truck, then remounted and gave a slight nod. With a click of his tongue, horse and rider trotted into the field behind her.

As he disappeared over the hill, Ann tried to brush off the wave of disappointment his absence brought. *I don't need him.* The wind whipped around her worn flannel sending a chill down her back. She climbed inside the truck and cranked the engine over. Shadows of low lying branches hovered over the road as the first signs of darkness crept in.

What was I thinking? I can't even turn this truck around on this narrow road and I'm headed in the wrong direction. And what wild critters was he talking about?

Her chest tightened around her lungs.

I should've asked for help.

♡♡♡

Jacob stayed out of sight long enough to determine her direction. Deep ditches lined the single-lane road. If she made an effort to turn around, he would still be close enough to give her a ride when she got stuck. He listened to the 350 engine cough as she drove further away before he nudged his gelding forward. Another pasture still needed hay for the cattle, and his children and dad would expect him home for dinner. Then he'd return and offer the obstinate woman the ride she stubbornly refused.

'Cause, she'll never make it across the creek.

He returned his gelding to the barn in exchange for the tractor. The side panel of the out-dated machine creaked as he opened it. A short hid itself somewhere in the wires of the starter. He wiggled them before turning the key.

The starter dragged indicating a low battery.

"I don't have time for this." He grabbed a can of starter fluid and sprayed the carburetor. Success. The engine turned over.

Jacob used the forks on the front to lift a large round bale of hay and drove to the north field. He deposited what he hoped would be the last bale needed for the season. If the predicted rains held their promise, he'd have more time to focus on other areas of the farm he'd neglected, such as the tractor that often didn't start. However, he'd lost two calves this spring already. The needed tractor parts depended on the sale of the calves. If he lost anymore, the parts would have to wait. Again.

Jacob climbed down from the old International and walked toward the edge of the field where buzzards were taking an interest. The evening sun had yet to fully set and call them to their nests. Ugly, black birds opened their wings and hissed violently at his intrusion. When he continued in their direction, they flew to a nearby tree, unwilling to stray far from their treasured find.

A calf.

Jacob stood over the carcass in disgust. The stench of its spoiled remains burned his nostrils. With the toe of his boot, he lifted the ear tag. The number confirmed what he expected. The calf had been missing for nearly a week, which explained the amount of decay.

But what got a hold of you, buddy?

The scavengers had erased all traces of the predator.

Jacob shoved his hands into the pockets of his jeans and trudged past the dead calf. Life continued to complicate itself, which left him strained in every direction. Where lines of laughter used to grace his eyes, now shadows of fatigue and doubt left their mark.

He shivered against the cold March wind and the memories that beckoned from the past. Today felt so similar to the one that constantly weighed on his mind. He wished for a change.

The field gave way to the river's edge, distracting him from his thoughts. The ever-changing waterways had stolen the glory of the Old Mill River. Reduced to a creek, it fought to make itself useful. The clear water trickled over smooth stones bringing a welcoming sense of peace.

He reached down to pick up a stone, but his attention halted at the sand by his feet. Jacob knelt and steadied himself with his hand. As he studied the imprinted clue, his stomach knotted with dread. Little satisfaction could be gained when it meant more trouble for livestock. He stood and raked his hard-worked hands through his hair.

The large four-toed track lacked claw marks.

Cougar.

Chapter Two

Jacob stepped through the backdoor unnoticed and sat on the nearby bench to slip off his boots. He watched his family and enjoyed the unguarded moment. The house hummed with the children's energy as they went about their chores. Ethan, being older, hovered over his sister.

"No, Sis. The napkins go under the forks, not on top," he grinned. Emily scrunched up her nose, before she changed all the place settings.

"I think I heard your dad come in." Their grandpa smiled over at Jacob as though he'd kept the secret long enough.

Jacob stood at the sound of his daughter's running feet and braced himself as Emily launched into his arms. He swung her small form above his head until she squealed with laughter then planted her back on the floor. Her long, tangled strawberry-blond hair bounced as she skipped around him.

Ethan walked over, imitating his father's posture. "The sow had her litter today, Dad. I counted seven of them."

"Did she have any trouble?"

He straightened his back a little more. "Nope, but I stuck around just in case."

Jacob's chest swelled with pride. His son exhibited a great maturity for eight-years-old. In the presence of his children, all stress from the farm would momentarily fade into the background.

"Daddy," Emily interrupted his thoughts, "can I hand-feed the runt?" Her light blue eyes sparkled with anticipation.

"You did that last time. It's your brother's turn now." He playfully tapped the end of her nose.

"Oh, pooh!" Emily pouted and stomped her foot.

Jacob smiled at her childish antics then turned to her brother. "And, Son, thanks for checking on the sow." He squeezed his shoulder as they started for the kitchen.

The kids seated themselves beside their grandpa, Luke, while Jacob washed at the kitchen sink. He appreciated the warm water as it relaxed his tired hands.

"Did you see any sign of what's gettin' the calves?" Luke shook his finger at Emily who tried to sneak a bite of her roll.

Jacob sighed. The stress hadn't gone far. It now knotted in his shoulders. "I think my first guess was right, Dad. That conservation agent can mock me all he wants, but I found the tracks to prove it today. We have a beef-fed cougar out there."

Jacob slipped the draped towel off the stove handle and dried his hands. The evening sky had already darkened and a low roll of thunder promised to wet his fields. Unfortunately, it would also wash away the track.

His only proof.

Luke shifted in his chair. "Let's not waste any time. We need to hunt it down before it kills any more livestock. What's the number at now, three that we've lost?"

"Four." Jacob stared out the kitchen window into the dark and contemplated the hunt. His children only had one parent to depend on and an aged grandfather. For their sakes, he couldn't afford unnecessary risks. "From what I've read, those cats are tricky. We should probably consider calling in some help."

He turned and faced his family. The children stared at him with huge, round eyes mixed with fear and excitement. He had to keep them safe. If something happened to them . . .Jacob settled in a seat beside Emily. "Kids," he made eye contact with both of them, "this means no more wandering around without Pa or me with you."

"Moses would keep me safe, Dad. When I go exploring, he never leaves my side." Ethan referred to his mutt who stood outside. His tail could be heard as it thumped the back door.

"That may be, but until I snag that cat, you're to do as I say. No need in taking any extra risk." Jacob paused and rubbed his chin. "Which makes me a bit worrisome for that lady I helped today."

Luke's brows rose. "What particular lady would that be?"

"The one with a flat tire and a high spirit." Though he spoke the words with affection, his forehead furled with concern. "And if my guess is right, she's wandering this way in the dark."

Outside, the sky rumbled to a steady rhythm. The thunder grew closer. With a cougar on the loose and a storm about to hit, that lonely road was no place for a woman. Before anyone could question him further, Jacob grabbed a dinner roll from the table, scooted back his chair and headed to the back door. He clenched the roll between his teeth as he slipped on his boots.

"You all go ahead without me. I'll be back in a bit with some company." He grabbed his coat and bolted out the door.

♡♡♡

Unease built in the pit of Ann's stomach the further away she drove. She glanced at the dash-board clock. Wobbly hands swayed back and forth across the six, keeping time with the truck's movements. Would she ever get back to her uncle's? As doubts tempted her to give up, she caught sight of an overgrown trail. She exhaled in relief and let her stomach muscles relax. "Thanks God. I was beginning to wonder if You'd forgotten I was out here."

Easing her foot off the gas pedal, she brought the truck to a slow stop past the trail. This time, she remembered to engage the clutch. She peered at the road ahead and noted the gravel disappeared into a wide creek. Her voice rose with each outspoken thought. "First I crossed a one-lane wooden bridge and now there's not even a bridge. Signs of civilization keep diminishing."

The stubborn stick shift refused to slide into reverse. "Oh, no you don't. I didn't come this far to give up now."

Ann returned the stick to neutral, lifted her foot from the clutch and shoved it down again. A trick she'd seen her uncle do. She pulled back toward reverse. After a few grinds from the transmission, it shifted into place. "Ha, I did it! Uncle Frank's farm, here I come."

She strained to see the road through the back window. *Here we go.* Peering over her shoulder, she turned the wheel to the left and pressed the gas to turn onto the path.

Crunch!

The tires dropped into a deep ditch, followed by the sound of the bumper as it dragged the gravel. Next, the increasingly familiar sound of a flattening tire hissed. Ann dropped her head forward onto the steering wheel. A rush of air left her lungs. Why couldn't this be a dream? "Uhhgg. I guess I should've finished that prayer about safety."

She swung open the door of the truck as a cool breeze swept in, tainted with the smell of rain. The fragrance would've been relaxing given different circumstances. Instead, goose bumps prickled across her skin. She shivered and reached behind the seat for the green army coat she saw earlier. It lacked a hood and boasted a broken zipper, but it would help.

She slipped it on. "Oh goodie, you and the jack must be roomies. You guys smell just alike." Sarcasm did little to improve her situation.

She stretched toward the glove box. "Please open." The rusted latch refused to budge. Banging on it didn't help either. At least, a partial moon imparted some light.

Sorry about the truck, Uncle Frank, but you left me a lemon.

Ann started back on the gravel road. How many miles was it to the cabin she'd passed? It didn't matter. Her only option was to walk. She pulled the coat tighter around her body, and tried to ward off nightmarish thoughts of what lurked about in the dark.

The largest animal she had to be concerned about was a coyote, and if she remembered correctly, they were mainly scavengers. She could throw her arms up in the air and make a lot of noise; that would probably scare them off. Or climb a tree. Maybe even sleep in one. Of course, the last time she climbed a tree she'd been fourteen. That was a far cry from twenty-seven. Could she even pull herself up in one now?

From the age of eight, she'd climbed every tree imaginable, often just to spy on her brother and his friends, wondering what could be so special she couldn't go along, too. It always gave her mother fits, afraid her only daughter would break her neck. But her aunt and uncle never minded.

That's why the acceptance of their invitation came so easily. While they vacationed, their farm became her personal retreat. If any place could distract her from the recent events in her life and help her relax, it would be here. The place that held her most treasured childhood memories.

Unfortunately, the drastic change had yet to prove enough. The all-too-real nightmares still haunted her sleep. She shivered and pulled the coat closer.

Ann paused and looked up at the starless sky. "I've waited for months to know what I'm supposed to do with my life, where I'm supposed to be." She inhaled a deep breath to ward off the urge to cry.

"What a sense of humor You must have, when You know that patience is anything but my strong suit." She often talked out-loud to God. "Life would be so much simpler if it came with a manual." The Bible came to mind. "I mean a personal one."

A sudden stillness settled around her. *Weren't there some frogs or night birds making noise a minute ago?*

The hairs on the back of her neck stood up. The leaves rustled off to her side. Ann jumped. "Ahh!"

The darkened form of a mouse scurried across the road and into the field.

Before she could laugh at her silly behavior a creature with a five-foot wingspan swooped overhead. Ann opened her mouth to scream, but all that came out was a hoarse whisper.

She froze in fear. Her breaths came in short gasps. As lightheadedness overwhelmed her, the terrible winged beast released its demonic laughter . . . in hoots.

"Hoot, hoot. Hoot, hoooooo."

Ann shook her head and nervously laughed at her own foolishness. Her chest heaved a huge sigh as she tried to slow the beating of her heart. She picked up her pace and continued down the road.

Though thankful she hadn't been in danger, she still couldn't shake the eerie feeling of being followed.

A shadow emerged in the field and mimicked her pace. Ann paused. Her breath froze on her lips. The shadow paused. Could this be what Jacob referred to, one of their wild critters? Tears of fear formed at the corner of her eyes. She stepped forward and quickened her stride. The shadow did the same.

Was it time to climb? Ann scanned the selection lining the road. Ahead three yards, stood a large tree with low branches. Her decision made, she took one last look toward the shadow . . . it turned into the field and disappeared in the night.

Thank you, God. Ann struggled to control the trembling in her legs. She had to keep walking. Besides, perhaps it was her imagination. It hadn't lessened with age, which made being a nanny so fitting. She allowed thoughts she'd tried to bury surface, anything to ward off her fears.

Her heart ached for the little girl and baby brother she'd no longer hold in her arms. She'd accepted them as she would've her own children. Although other nannies had warned her to protect her heart, stay at a distance, Ann couldn't. She'd always been an all or nothing kind of girl.

A few yards further, her foot slipped on loose gravel. She lurched forward and braced her fall with her hands, but not before her knee took the blunt of the impact.

"Oh, no," Ann moaned and turned over to see the damage. "Great, this jacket won't zip, and now I've torn my jeans and everything is throbbing." Her exaggerated moan preceded a loud crash of thunder.

♡♡♡

Jacob pulled his pickup out of the lean-to as it began to rain. *That lady's mood is going to be even prettier.* After a quick decision, he turned down the way he'd last seen her. He figured her spare wouldn't have held out long enough to get past his place.

His dad would have his hands full with the children. They rarely received visitors and their excitement was clearly evident in their bright eyes.

A pang of guilt settled in his chest. He sighed and peered through the window, forcing himself to see more than his past. Since their mother left, he'd allowed himself to grow cynical and cold toward the idea of ever pursuing another relationship. He still didn't know where he went wrong by his ex-wife but sure didn't want to fail again. Although that decision suited him fine, his children were the ones who suffered. Their grandmother had passed away a year before, which left them lacking a female's touch. Luke did his best to fill in, but a man could only provide so much.

The odds didn't look good for Emily. As if her hair wasn't already an indication.

Why, he didn't know, but Ann's face came to mind. Though her safety still posed a concern, he gave in to the tiny smile that tugged at the corners of his mouth. *She sure looked nice in those snug jeans.*

What would it be like to have a wife with that kind of spunk? Fun and challenging. The kind of challenge a man looks forward to.

He considered his past marriage. Something could be said for marrying someone for comfort. It might sound okay, but it's never enough. Maybe if they had waited to have children, lived a little, fought a little, played a lot. But why think about a past he couldn't change?

About a mile and a half down the road he spotted her. She made a pitiful sight with her damp hair, a noticeable limp, and what—did she just hunker down in the ditch? He arched a brow. Was she hiding?

Jacob slowed his truck to a stop in the middle of the road, leaving the windshield wipers thumping in a steady rhythm. He stepped out and advanced toward Ann through the pouring rain. He saw her open her mouth and swung her up in his arms. "Save it, I'm not getting soaked to the bone just to hear you yammer."

He came off gruff, but had no appreciation for ice cold rain down his back. Besides that, he found it easier to aggravate this spunky lady than face the growing awareness she caused. She smelled like sweet honeysuckle that grew along the roadside in the spring.

His favorite scent.

And with each forward stride, her head fell against his chest while her hands tightened around his shoulders. He warmed to the feel of her in his arms. And when she shivered, he did exactly what he'd wanted to, he drew her closer.

What's happening to me?

This vulnerable woman was breaching the very barriers he'd so carefully erected.

The rain increased and the sky thundered in rhythm as Jacob reached the truck. He threw open the door and thrust Ann over to the middle of the seat as he quickly followed. She tried to scoot to the other door but couldn't. Farm supplies occupied the seat. After he flipped the heater fan to max, he threw his arm across the back of the seat. "We'll have to drive in reverse. Your truck is blocking the only turn around."

Jacob marveled at the way she held her composure. He suspected he unnerved her and fully expected a mouthful once they were inside the truck, but to his amazement, this whirlwind of a woman sat silent. "Are you frozen?"

Ann shot him a quick glance. "A little cold . . . and a little tired of walking."

Not one to say, I told you so, he didn't respond to her admission. "Hold your hands to the vent. You need the heat more than me."

Jacob dared to look in her direction and noted she even appeared humble. With her torn jeans and soggy clothes and hair, she looked bedraggled and lost. He mentally fought off the growing urge to stop the truck and hold her. With one more stolen glance, this time at her dewy lips, he mentally confessed he'd never be able to stop with an embrace.

Where are these thoughts coming from?

He forced his attention back to the road and tried to further dampen his desires with the acknowledgment she'd never let him touch her. As she warmed, her defiant streak took control again as though convincing her she no longer needed his help. She now leaned forward, probably in an effort to keep their bodies from touching.

Well if that's the case, he'd have to improvise.

Jacob gave in to his mischievous thought and let the truck lurch, which threw Ann against the back of the seat. He smiled out of the side of his mouth. "Now that's the way you're supposed to sit."

Since he still drove in reverse, Jacob eased passed his driveway and slowed to a stop then shifted forward and turned toward his cabin.

Ann jerked her head toward him, anxiety lacing every word. "I thought you were taking me home?"

"Not in this weather, I—"

"I can't stay here," she interrupted. "I need to get back to my uncle's house. I assumed you would realize that."

Jacob's gaze fell to where her hand rested on his forearm, sending sparks clear to his heart. She quickly withdrew her hand and stared at the floor of the cab

"Look Lady, if we can even make it across the wooden bridge I'd be surprised, but just supposing we could, I'd never get back over it before the flood waters. So the way I see it, I have two options. I can either be stuck at your place, excuse me, your uncle's place, or you can be stuck at mine. And, I believe my kids would like me home."

Ann slowly brought her head up and narrowed a gaze at Jacob. "*You*, have children?"

Chapter Three

Ann's curiosity grew as they approached the back of the cabin. Jacob pulled to a stop but kept the truck running. The rain pounded around them and made it hard to hear his voice. "Go on in, I'll be right there."

He helped her out then returned to the cab. She stepped around the truck before he drove away to park and nearly fell again as her right foot sank into a deep hole, filling her boot with water.

"Ahh, that's freezing!" She hurried toward the house, thankful she didn't have far to walk.

Ann hovered beneath the small shelter overhanging the door. As a stranger, did she go in and perhaps frighten the children, or disobey the "ego" man's instructions and get soaked? Puffs of air could be seen in front of her from the warmth of her breath meeting the cold air. Her foot grew numb. Perhaps she should take the risk.

Someone made the decision for her as the door swung open and an aged hand pulled her through by the arm. An older version of Jacob stood in the threshold and stepped back to allow her room to enter.

"My, don't you look like a wet puppy dog." The man smiled. A young boy of about eight and a little girl of four or five stood on either side with wide smiles.

"Hi, I . . ." Ann's explanation stalled on her tongue at the sight of the little girl. Her resemblance to the one she had to leave clenched her heart. She'd still be her nanny if the girl's dad hadn't–*No, I'm not going there.*

"You're pretty even if you're a wet dog," giggled the girl. Jacob interrupted her laughter as he threw open the door and collided with Ann.

"Whoa, are you all right?" Jacob caught Ann around the middle and twirled her around to face him.

Anger welled inside her at the sight of his crooked smile. Would this man ever get tired of making her uncomfortable? As she drew her eyes up to meet his, she mellowed.

There, if only for a moment, she caught him unguarded. His eyes had taken on a softness that had earlier been absent. Perhaps there was more to this man than he let on. The feel of his protective hands supporting her waist added to the depth in his eyes, softened her heart. Also, the burning feeling returned in her stomach. Her brain told her to flee, but her flesh rejoiced.

The older man stepped around them to shut the door. "I'll get some towels, 'cause you two's gonna need 'em."

Ann moved away from Jacob's hold, though her side still burned from his touch and acknowledged the children. They smiled eagerly.

The boy extended his hand. "Hi. I'm Ethan, and that was Pa, and this is—"

Before he could introduce the girl, the storm reminded them of its presence. The rain poured down in sheets. A bright bolt of lightning lit up the sky and the small girl jumped into Jacob's arms. He laughed and tried to pull her arms loose from around his neck.

"Honey, you're going to be soaked."

"I don't care, Daddy, I'm not gonna let that storm get me—I mean you."

Ann blinked against the stinging of tears. The family made a beautiful scene, something she'd always wanted but accepted she'd never have.

Jacob smiled and gently sat her down. "Now we both need to get some dry clothes.

He looked over at Ann, but she read his initial intentions. Then a softened curiosity colored his gaze. Had he noticed her emotional slip?

Ann dropped her chin and shifted her weight from her cut knee. "I'm fine. My coat took the worst of it."

He glanced past her coat. "I'd have to argue that. It looks to me like your hands and knee took the worst."

She had to acknowledge Jacob was right. Her hands were a mess, and bits of gravel embedded her knee.

Jacob shifted to the bench. "Let's leave our shoes here, and then we'll get you cleaned up."

"Oh, I can manage on my own if you'll just show me a sink." In an attempt to keep her courage, Ann avoided Jacob's eyes.

He didn't answer, and Ann knew she was on losing ground. If she wanted an opinion at all around this man, she would have to fight for it.

Ann sat beside Jacob and struggled to untie the soaked laces of her hiking boots. Not only were her fingers numb, but her abrasions burned with each movement. Jacob reached over and deftly finished the job then gave her a polite nod of his head. For the first time, true gratitude sprang up inside her for his help. As she removed her boots and socks, the children giggled.

"Looks like you could wring a river out of that." The grandpa teased as he pointed to the cause of the children's laughter, her dripping sock.

"I think I stepped in a hole out there." Ann smiled back at the amused faces and pointed toward the door.

Jacob reached over and took the wet socks from her hand. He stood and tossed them by the wood stove. "They'll be dry soon enough. Emily, you get some dry clothes on. Ann, you can follow me."

Ann raised her brows and wrinkled her forehead as she looked toward the older man, but he only smiled.

Jacob crowded the sink in the tight-quartered bathroom. She had only been a few steps behind but he already had the water running and disinfectant at hand. After he washed up, he turned to her. "Let's see the damage."

Ann stood as far back as she could, which wasn't much, given the lack of space. She held out her hands and tried to keep as much distance from the bewildering stranger as possible. Jacob reached for her wrists and pulled her to him, which caused her body to lightly bump against his.

Sparks flew.

"I can see better under the light." His deep voice had a way of rumbling that seemed to ricochet off her heart. She resented the reaction.

"You're enjoying this, aren't you?" Ann clenched her teeth behind tight lips and tried to fight the tide of emotions that rocked against her core.

He kept his attention on her hands. "If you mean having to go out after a cantankerous and stubborn lady in the middle of a thunderstorm and getting myself soaked, then I'd have to disagree."

Silence fell between them. His hand rubbed across her palm, his soft touch sent a pleasing sensation through Ann. Did he feel it too?

She studied his profile as he continued to brush the dirt from her hand. When he lifted his gaze to hers, she couldn't turn away, but felt the heat of a blush creeping up her neck. His assured smile caused her to divert her eyes to the sink. She'd been caught. But what did that matter? It didn't mean anything. Did it?

His calloused hands finished cleaning her abrasions with a ginger touch. He took his time as though he didn't want to cause her any extra pain. She wished the medicine was as thoughtful.

"Ouch, that stings!"

"Alcohol does that." He blew over her hands. "So toughen up, because from the look of blood on your jeans, your knee's going to be a lot worse."

Ann glanced down and grimaced. Jacob was right, yet again. *This is getting tiresome.* As soon as she let the thought loose, guilt riddled her conscience. Jacob had changed her tire, came back for her in a storm, and now helped to clean and bandage her cuts. True, he was arrogant and at times condescending, but who was she to complain? If only she could hold on to that grateful attitude throughout the evening, she might be able to put up with him.

"Now trade me spots, and you can sit while I take a look at your knee."

Ann knew any amount of rebuttal would be met head on, so she complied and proceeded to move around Jacob's bulk. The small size of the bathroom caused their bodies to graze against each other as they switched places.

Fireworks danced inside like the fourth of July. She peered up at Jacob. The contact wasn't lost on him, either. His eyes darkened and grew more intense. Desire beckoned her to give in to his stare. Ann could feel her body will itself toward him. It didn't make any sense. What was wrong with her flesh, and why didn't she fight against it?

Her knee made contact with the cabinet of the basin and pain flared at the site of her cut. She gasped and blinked away any tears. Jacob guided her by the arms and helped her sit, then turned his attention to her knee. He placed his fingers on either side of the rip of her jeans.

Did he intend to tear them further? She grasped his hands to stop him. "Don't. This is all I have with me." Just as quickly, she pulled them back, startled by the powerful electricity that sizzled between them. "I can pull them over my knee."

His steady gaze bore through her. There was no denying the fact, he felt it too. "I'm not so sure, but sit back and I'll give it a try."

Jacob balanced on the balls of his feet and placed his hand under her calf muscle. He raised her leg so her foot sat in his lap. Cautious, he pulled up the hem of her jeans to examine the cut. Ann's bare foot left her leg more exposed. As if to add to her vulnerability, she noticed Jacob observe the shape of her leg then trail his eyes down the short length of her foot

I'm glad I painted my toe nails. She inwardly cringed. *No, I mean I shouldn't have. I don't want him attracted to me. Right?*

He'd replaced his hand beneath her leg and allowed it to follow his gaze.

Ann searched her heart for signs of alarm but couldn't find any past the feel of excitement as it coursed through her veins. Still, for the sake of control, she pursed her lips to scold him, but when he looked up her mouth went dry. Jacob's eyes grew determined as his hand continued back up her leg. He leaned forward just as Emily's voice broke the spell.

"Is she hurt very badly, Daddy?"

He kept his gaze on Ann and replied without turning around. "She'll be fine, Hon'. We'll be out in a minute." Satisfied, Emily skipped toward the kitchen to wait with Ethan and Grandpa.

Jacob cleared his throat and shifted his focus back to Ann's knee. He released a low whistle. "You did a number on this one. Looks like you caught a sharp piece of shale." Giving his tongue a click he added, "Hold your breath, 'cause you've got some gravel in it, too."

Ann usually prided herself on her level of pain tolerance, but with the uncertainty of her future looming over her, coupled with the disastrous events of the day, exhaustion claimed her convincing front. As Jacob dabbed at her knee with the wet cloth, she flinched with each movement.

He looked up in time to see a tear escape her lower lashes. Quickly, so as to beat him to it, Ann swiped it away with the back of her hand. Her flesh had already proven unreliable and if she had to stay here for the night, she'd have to limit as much physical contact as possible from this intriguing man.

Jacob stood and reached toward the medicine cabinet. "Your cut could use some stitches," Ann's quick intake of air caused him to pause. "But since we're in the predicament we're in, we'll just use some tape. It's what we do in place of stitches out here, and it always works fine."

Ann nodded. She could only hope he would forget about the alcohol. As he knelt back on the floor, Jacob again propped her foot against his thigh. He appeared reluctant at first, but soon resumed his task and administered the disinfectant.

Her knee felt like it doubled in size as the burning sensation ignited every nerve. Ann clasped Jacob's broad shoulder. "Blow, blow, blow!"

Jacob blew on her cut in between his erupting smiles then finished with the tape and gauze. He gently pulled the leg of her jeans back down and reached over with his right hand to take hers from his shoulder. He stood, pulled Ann to her feet, and with a husky voice asked, "All better?"

Frustrated at the ease in which he made her speechless, she commanded her voice to respond, though barely audible. "Yes, thank you."

His steady gaze bore through her. She grew uncomfortable and tried to pull her hand from his warm grasp.

Jacob held on to hers. "We'll keep a check on it, and I'll replace the gauze in the morning."

Was he trying to make a point she was staying with him tonight? He released her hand and turned down the hall to change into dry clothes.

Stunned, Ann stood alone for a moment before moving. What was she supposed to interpret from all of this? Jacob's advances, if they were indeed that, were unlike any she had ever experienced. As a waitress, and unfortunately, also as a nanny, she learned how to read men's intentions fairly well, or so she thought. She tried to shake off her bewilderment and focus on the grandfather. His presence would keep a balance to all of this.

Chapter Four

The children's grandpa had two plates prepared when Ann returned to the kitchen. "I figured after your exciting evening you could use something warm in your belly. Have a seat by me, and I'll sip my coffee while you tell me and the kids all about yourself."

Ann looked around and bit her bottom lip. There was no rescue this time. She complied with the sweet, older gentleman and took the offered seat. Ethan seated himself across from her and his sister sat on the edge of her grandpa's lap, her face beaming.

"You're real pretty. What's your name? Mine's Emily, and I'm four." Emily held out four stubby fingers in an attempt to draw further attention to her proud age.

Ann laughed softly. "You're also quite beautiful. I bet you keep a constant energy in this house." She appreciated the conversation resting on Emily for the moment, unaware of Jacob as he entered from the hall.

His voice startled her when he spoke. "That she does, but I'm afraid you've not answered her question. We'd all like to know who, exactly, you are."

A dark blue pullover blanketed his chest and heightened the intensity of his blue eyes, which at that particular moment pinned Ann to her chair. "You mentioned an uncle but never gave his name."

Ann cleared her throat and shifted uncomfortably in her chair. "I'm Ann McHaven. My aunt and uncle are the Garrets that live just off the highway."

She returned his accusing stare with false confidence, as though his authoritative demeanor had no effect.

"I've met them. But why were you driving down this road? Have you ever tried crossing the creek before?"

Ann's gaze dropped to the floor. "No. I was only going for a drive, and the road looked appealing."

In typical four-year old fashion, Emily interrupted the would-be interrogation with enthusiasm. "Daddy lets me stay up late when it's stormy!"

"Only for a little while." Jacob's baritone voice rumbled with affection as he gave a loving glance toward his daughter.

Ethan leaned forward, interested in joining the conversation. Or so it seemed. "Ma'am, did you hear anything following you while you were out there?"

Ann breathed a sigh of relief, thankful for the children and their skill at moving conversations forward. "Unfortunately, just the wind and the rain, and they caught up with me." She smiled as she touched her wet hair.

"Oh, and an owl." She waved off the comment as though it were nothing. She didn't want to give way to her momentary fear and have to explain her wild imagination.

"Well, Dad says we have a cougar eating our calves and we hoped you wouldn't meet up with him."

Ann's mouth dropped. She hadn't expected this turn of the conversation. Did that explain the shadow and her feeling of being followed? Goose-bumps trailed down her arms. She turned toward Jacob then his father. "Is he serious?"

"Yep, my son found the tracks this morning." He nodded toward Jacob, for him to continue.

"Maybe you'll keep that in mind, next time you decide to run around in a truck with rotted tires." He pushed off the wall where he'd leaned and crossed his arms over his broad chest.

"I beg your pardon, but . . ." Ann wanted nothing more than to tell him off, but remembered her young audience and settled for mumbling, "There won't be a next time. I can assure you."

Jacob's dad cut into the tension. "Your dinners are going to get cold if we keep this up. Go ahead and eat, and we can talk more tomorrow." He kissed the children on top of their heads and ambled toward the door where he pulled on his coat and boots. "Well, I'd best be going and check on Candy while there's a lull in the storm. You know how fearful she gets."

Ann spun around in her chair. Her frightened eyes pinned on the older man. "You're coming back, right?"

"Tomorrow, sure, but I've got my own place." He smiled gently. Had he picked up on her anxiety?

"You couldn't be in better hands, honey, and Candy's an old dog who needs reassuring. Kind of like that little one right beside you." He glanced at Emily before he turned to talk with Jacob who had joined him at the door.

Ann felt the room shrink. The grandpa had eased her discomfort with his gentle manner. Where Jacobs's eyes were probing and intense, his father's drew down at the corners and his brows went upward like a rooftop, which gave him an honest and amiable appearance. Without his presence she felt vulnerable around Jacob. He had a way of getting what he wanted. His children obeyed his first command. Even Ann, caught herself quiet and obedient toward him some of the time, for which she definitely had an aversion.

What if he expected something more of her? And where would she sleep? The cabin was bigger than she first assumed, but aside from the couch, she guessed there to be only two bedrooms.

She drew in a deep breath, refused her mind anymore worries, and turned her attention to Emily. "Do storms keep you restless as well?"

"Uh-huh." Emily's eyes widened as she nodded her head. "I can't sleep 'cause I get scared." She paused and smiled. "Miss Ann, I bet I could sleep better if you'd read me a story."

Ann fully enjoyed being around the innocence of children again. The worst part of losing her nanny position had been leaving the children. "I'll do better than that. How about I sing you a song that tells you how to be brave during storms?"

"You can do that?" Emily whispered.

"You bet. But you *will* need a teddy bear."

With the exception of the cougar story, Ethan had been reserved most of the evening as if assessing Ann's motives. He probably had to grow up a bit faster than his sister, since there didn't seem to be a mother present.

Their mother's no concern of yours, Ann. Remember what you've been told, "Don't get attached." She twirled a strand of hair. *But every child needs a mother.*

She paused and let her mind wonder. *And then there's Jacob, apparently without a wife.*

Emily ran down the hall and Ethan moved from his place at the table. "I think I'll go to bed now, too."

Jacob shut the door as his father left. The sound echoed like a final note in her mind. *Don't do anything to lead him on.* Thoughts of their shared electricity returned and made her stomach churn. *I think it's too late for that.*

Jacob turned to Ethan. "You and your sister will sleep in my room tonight."

Ann's shoulders tensed. Where did that leave her?

"And we'll let Ann have you kids' room and Em's bed."

Emily emerged from her room and held a bedraggled brown bear with a pink ribbon around its neck. She ran to Ann and clasped her hand and giggled. "Come on, I'll show you Daddy's room. I get to sleep in the *big* bed!"

Unable to stop the force of excitement from this one little girl, Ann could only give Jacob a brief glimpse over her shoulder with hopes he understood she wasn't purposefully intruding into his private space. Inside, Ann noticed the *huge bed*, which had been Em's delight, was only a full size mattress set on a simple frame. The small room only had space for one large dresser and a night stand. How could any woman have ever lived here?

She made her way to the side of the bed. Emily giggled and jumped under the covers with her bear. As Ann sat down, another bolt of lightning lit up the sky in view from the small window on the opposite wall. Emily jumped into Ann's lap and wrapped her arms around her neck. Though surprised by the child's instant trust, Ann savored the moment and returned the embrace. She allowed it to ease the ache in her heart for the girl she had to leave behind before settling her back on the bed.

"It's all right, Emily. Hold your teddy tight while I sing, okay?"

Emily's response faded in the background, as movement by the doorway stole Ann's attention. Ethan shuffled inside but hesitated before going further.

Ann gently smiled. "Emily would probably feel better if you were beside her." Though it was likely she'd never see the children again, she still wanted this young man to trust her.

"All right." Ethan's shoulders relaxed as if relieved by her offer. He casually walked to the other side. His desire to exhibit his father's confidence was obvious. But when he climbed onto the bed, Ann caught sight of the tattered stuffed animal half-way concealed under his arm.

Memories of her childhood surfaced. A fluffy pink rabbit with ears as long as its body always shared her bed. Each parent would come in to say good-night and tuck her in. Her youth had been full of security and love. Would she ever have that again?

She glanced at each child now nestled in their father's bed. They seemed to enjoy the same type of childhood, only they lacked a mother. As she sang, her heart twisted for the precious children.

♡♡♡

Jacob quietly listened from outside the door and relished the beauty of what unfolded. His children felt secure with Ann. Her voice held a simple purity that could easily erase their fears. He allowed himself to relax with one shoulder against the wall as he closed his eyes and listened.

Chapter Five

Ann stepped into the hallway and collided with Jacob. She threw her hand to his chest to stop her momentum and blushed with embarrassment. "Oh, I didn't know you were there."

She slowly let her hand drop from his hard, muscled frame. Her breath hitched and her heart kept an erratic beat.

Jacob broke the ensuing silence and cleared his throat. "Why don't you grab a bite to eat and I'll tell the children goodnight."

Unable to speak, Ann dutifully obeyed. Why hadn't she moved her hand faster? *How embarrassing.* The reason was clear, however. The feel of her hand touching against his warm, firm chest was exciting. Vibrant sparks had danced between them like camp fire embers shooting skyward.

Ann shook her head. Her wishing had always landed her too high in the clouds. In an effort to keep her feet on the ground she reminded herself of her past experiences with men.

As a waitress, she hadn't met an overwhelming amount of gentlemen. Flirting for tips had a way of back-firing. That much she'd learned. Hands would find their way to places they didn't belong and lustful insinuations were the norm. Once Ann realized they were only responding to the message being sent she changed, but being more professional would take a different crowd.

Thankful for a way out, another opportunity had presented itself and she willingly accepted. Though being a nanny hadn't proven to be the answer either. Guilt filled her conscience. Had she flirted with him, too? Is that why—

As though it were meant to drive her negative thoughts away, she heard Emily's voice in a loud whisper, "Can we keep her, Daddy?"

Ann hurried to the kitchen to busy herself so Jacob wouldn't notice the effect he had on her. He sent her nerve endings into overdrive. She should at least be somewhat afraid. Instead, a growing intensity, not at all related to fear, threatened to overwhelm her. Unable or unwilling to sort through her feelings, Ann picked up a wet glass from the strainer and proceeded to dry it. She imagined Jacob's dad would be disappointed to see their dinners sat cold, but her nerves had stolen her appetite.

The back of Ann's neck tingled. Jacob had reentered the room. She turned and found him watching her. "I'm sorry if I overstepped any boundaries . . ."

Jacob closed the distance between them and Ann's knees lost their strength. She grasped the counter's edge for support. His fingers brushed against hers as he took the glass from her hand. "If you keep drying this, you're going to break it. And I don't think those fragile hands need another beating." Their hands still touched as he spoke.

Ann fought to keep her balance and finally broke her gaze from his as she looked down at their hands and swallowed. She quickly withdrew hers and rubbed one palm over the back of the other. "I just wanted to help clean up." She stepped back. "If you don't mind, I think I'll call it a night, too."

Jacob looked at the full dinner plates. The steak and fried potatoes sat cold and unappealing. "You're not hungry?"

"No. It was nice of your father, but maybe we could just wrap my plate and put it in the fridge."

"Alright, I'll take care of it and you can head off." Ann was sure she detected disappointment in his voice. "You'll find a night shirt on Em's bed for you."

Her eyebrows shot upward. "Thank you."

Where would he sleep? She didn't want to step onto personal ground, but for her own peace of mind, she needed to know where this man would be during the night. "Umm, you're not going to sleep on the floor are you?"

"Don't worry about me." He placed his hand in the small of her back and escorted her to the children's room.

As Ann was about to step through the doorway a loud crack of thunder sounded as if it would split the sky open. Ann jumped and let go of a small cry of surprise.

Jacob leaned against the door jam and smiled. "So, you and Emily have something in common."

Ann jutted her chin forward. "I'm not afraid of storms." He didn't look convinced. "The loud sound just startled me. I'm sure it did you, too."

Jacob slowly shook his head. "You didn't see me jump."

His lazy smirk broadened into a grin.

Ann jumped again as the sound repeated itself, and hung her head. "Okay, so I startle easily. No big deal," she said, as she unsuccessfully tried to hide her smile.

"Good night, Ann." His voice had taken on a husky attractiveness.

She stepped further inside and turned to see where Jacob had placed himself. He remained in the doorway; his imposing frame filled most of it. His wide chest heaved outward as he took in a deep breath before pulling the door closed. Ann finally allowed herself to breathe and looked toward the bed to find the shirt.

"Don't be so silly, he's no different than the others." Ann tried to talk sense into the emotions that played hopscotch inside her.

She picked up the well washed shirt by the hanger and assumed it must be one of Jacob's, a light blue cotton button down, several sizes too big but comfortable to snuggle in. No longer willing to restrain herself, Ann drew the shirt to her face and inhaled Jacob's scent.

♡♡♡

Jacob continued to stand outside the door and fought the urge to step inside. "God help me," he absently pleaded. He'd never battled such strong feelings of attraction before. What was wrong with him? He was around other women every week with church and town. Why should this particular woman be any different? It didn't make sense. There were at least three others who had made it clear they were interested, yet they didn't move him in the slightest. And it wasn't because they weren't attractive. He simply didn't see the need to complicate his life any further.

The fact that he even considered stepping inside her room alarmed him. Though he no longer talked to God, he still held to his Christian upbringing. There was an obvious difference between right and wrong. And the tantalizing thoughts that invaded his mind were definitely wrong.

If only her eyes hadn't revealed the same.

Jacob threw cold water on his face at the bathroom sink in hopes it would clear his mind. It didn't. Giving up, he put away both plates of food and joined his kids in the bedroom. A blanket and pillow tossed on the floor offered little comfort.

Two hours crept by. Either he'd become soft, or the floor was harder than he remembered. Uncomfortable and restless from his thoughts, he shuffled to the living room and surrendered to the couch.

Ann awakened places in him that'd been asleep too long. As if her spunky personality didn't appeal to him enough, he found her strikingly beautiful. Her small frame held perfectly balanced curves that were accented by long, copper colored hair. And her bewitching, hazel eyes told of her every mood.

His mind came to rest on Ann standing at the sink. That was the moment he knew he wanted her. He wanted her here to sing to his children, to find her at home in his house and to feel her next to him. Before he had the chance to consider the speed his thoughts were moving, he remembered Ann mentioned life had been insulting. An unexpected feeling rose in his chest. Had someone hurt her? He clenched his jaw. Was it a boyfriend? Jacob considered the notion and didn't like it at all.

♡♡♡

The clock struck midnight as Ann turned over and stared at the door. Would she ever fall asleep? Though fear of her returning nightmare often kept her awake, tonight there were other parts to the equation. Such as the all too interesting feelings toward her rescuer. As disturbing as Jacob was, he was also equally appealing. Why? This was completely new ground. Of course she'd dated throughout the years, but no one's touch had ever ignited an instant cascade of emotions like tonight's experience.

Frustrated by her circular thinking and quite aware it wasn't producing any answers, Ann contemplated getting up. *It's quiet. Everyone must be asleep, so it shouldn't matter if I slip into the kitchen for a drink.* Although her borrowed night shirt hung to her knees, she still didn't want to be seen in it. But if she were quick, she'd make it back to her room without being seen.

Ann peered down the hall. The dim lighting of a nightlight mingled with the quiet hush of the sleeping house. With delicate tiptoes, she entered the kitchen. She filled the glass that Jacob last touched but never brought it to her lips. The image of his hands touching hers brought a wry smile to her mouth. *If his hands cause that much excitement, I wonder what his lips do.*

"Couldn't sleep?" A mocking baritone voice called from the living room.

Ann flinched and spun around. Water spilled down the side of her shirt and leg. If the burning of her cheeks were any indication, she was beet red at this point. Guilt spread through her. What right did she have to think like that? Leading a stranger on while stuck in his home was the last thing she needed to do. *Clean up your thoughts, Ann, and your actions will be clean.*

"Wh- what are you doing in here? I- I thought you were with the kids."

"The floor was too hard, or maybe I'm getting soft." Jacob's hand rubbed the back of his neck as he advanced toward her and removed a towel from the drawer.

Ann tensed and kept her eyes on his every move. He wore the same clothes as earlier. Only now his shirt hung loose, which made him appear even taller. Was he considering blotting her shirt and leg? *He'd better not try.*

Jacob wiped the floor, the muscles in his arm flexed with each movement. Ann pulled her thoughts away from his body and concentrated on his generosity. Experience taught her most men would've watched as she cleaned up. But not Jacob—her host, the Pandora box. He flipped the towel onto the counter.

Ann's eyes darted from him to the counter. She breathed a sigh of relief then tossed her hair behind her shoulder and raised her glass. "This is all I needed, so good night again." She stepped aside to go around Jacob when he took hold of her elbow and guided her to a kitchen chair. He tossed her the towel. "You and I both know you can't sleep, so stop with the charade and we'll have some coffee."

When Jacob says jump, does someone always respond how high? The thing that irritated her most was that this time she was the puppet. She considered arguing the fact she needed her jeans, but knew she'd be met with his stubbornness. Thus, she opted for drawing the least amount of attention to her legs by remaining silent and slid them under the table.

Jacob turned back to the counter to heat their coffee. "I know most of the families who live around here, including the Garretts, but I've not heard of any McHavens."

"That's because my parents still reside in Illinois." He waited for her to elaborate. "My aunt is originally from there as well, but when she met Uncle Carl she moved out here with him."

"How long have you been staying there?"

"Is this the interrogation you wanted to start earlier?" Her smart-aleck attitude resurfaced.

Now it was his turn to eye her warily as he turned from the counter. "Are you trying to avoid answering the question?"

With a defeated sigh, Ann said, "I've been here for two months." An idea formed in her mind. She bit back a smile and led him down a rabbit trail for her own humor.

"After my release, it was agreed that I would spend the rest of my parole in this area, and with good conduct I can finish my sentence early." Pleased, she sat back to admire her work and waited for Jacob's response.

Jacob's eyes held a gleam she couldn't place. "You'll want to work hard at that. I didn't, and it cost me an extra five years."

Ann dropped her jaw. The beat of her heart stalled as all warmth drained from her body.

Jacob's smirk exploded into hearty laughter. "Surely you've figured out I can see right through you. You may as well spill your guts, so to speak, or we'll never get through this *interrogation*."

Ann drew a deep breath, grateful air could reenter her lungs and accepted the coffee Jacob offered. So, the man had a sense of humor. She'd have to work hard to stay one step ahead of him. Though that would be difficult, considering his every touch brought with it an absence of rational thought. Which didn't make any sense at all knowing what she was in Missouri to recuperate from. Fear is what she would've expected, not the pull of attraction.

She sat her cup down and leaned on the table as her hair spilled over one shoulder. "Like I said, I've been here for two months," she played with one of her curls. "I came to visit for a while and my uncle asked if I'd house sit while they took an overdue vacation."

"Hmmm. Two months is a long visit. What were you doing before you came here?" He seated himself in front of her.

She froze. Pictures of her past shot through her mind like snapshots. Her employer. His silhouette in her doorway. His body hovered over hers. Her hands pushed against his chest. His horror-stricken wife.

She shuddered and steered Jacob away from personal ground.

"All these questions are ridiculous. My knee's getting stiff and I'm tired." Ann meant to rise, but Jacob blocked her legs with his and grabbed her ankles with his hand.

"You need to stretch your leg out." He lifted her feet onto his lap.

Her eyes narrowed. "And I think your being too possessive with my legs."

With his cup paused at his lips, he raised an eyebrow. "I think you'd agree, better your legs than your body."

Ann fidgeted with her coffee cup. He made it clear he was attracted to her. So if conversation is what he wanted, then at least it was safe ground.

He smiled and took a sip of coffee.

"I was a nanny. I cared for a little girl named Amy. She's a year younger than your Emily." Her gaze drifted to the wall behind Jacob, seeing nothing, then refocused. Though the unpredictable man in front of her made her feel uncomfortable, she didn't fear him. But she still protected her secrets. "Now, I'm deciding what I want to do next."

Jacob listened intently and absently massaged her feet. Ann squirmed once when he touched a tickle spot. "Does anyone know of your whereabouts tonight?"

Softly, she replied, "No."

"Is there anyone we can contact that might call to check on you, like a friend or a neighbor?"

"I didn't think of a neighbor," she said, as she unsuccessfully tried to retrieve her legs. "Mr. Whitener may. He's a good friend to my uncle. I'm sure my family won't call. I'm usually the one to call them, and they won't be expecting another call until next week."

Oh! Why am I telling him of all this? Yet again, she became the all too trusting girl next door and inadvertently gave out more information than needed. She hoped he didn't have a motive to use it against her and searched for a change of topic.

"Are you a farmer?" Ann twirled a strand of hair waiting for her host to answer.

Jacob's steady gaze fixed on hers as he ignored her question. "No one knows where you are or where to look?"

His question alarmed her. What if she'd been wrong? What devious plans might he be contemplating?

Chapter Six

Ann squirmed in her seat. Had she misread him? "Just what are you implying?"

"Usually when the creeks get up it's days before we can get out again. I thought we should contact somebody tomorrow to let them know where you are."

Partially relieved by his temporary innocence, Ann studied his face before she replied. She wanted to gauge his motives correctly but finally had to step out on faith, unable to read past his calm, yet probing stare. *Lord, protect me, I want to trust this man.*

"I guess we could call Mr. Whitener." She pulled her eyes from Jacob to look around the room. Pine cabinets and vacant walls surrounded her. "Do you even have a phone?"

"No, don't have a need. When the weather gets like this my neighbors, the Stevenson's, meet me by the creek and check on us. We have it smoothed down to a certain time, and it works just fine."

The name sounded familiar but Ann couldn't place them right off. "If we do call, where do I tell him I'm at? I don't even know your last name."

"It's Durham, Jacob Durham. I guess we left out the formalities earlier. Luke's my dad, and I think my kids made themselves known." As he spoke, his eyes sparkled at the mention of his family. *Oh, to have a man that appreciates his family.* Though she had a quiver of doubt about him earlier, it wasn't strong enough to override the attraction that now pulled at her.

"So you're all alone." His last statement settled like a brick. She was alone and had been for longer than she ever imagined. Unable to meet his eyes she silently nodded her head in agreement as she pictured the empty farmhouse that awaited her. When her stay there was over, she didn't even have an apartment to go home to.

Surely it was a gesture of sympathy that caused him to take her hand. But when Jacob gave it a gentle squeeze, it immediately brought her back to the present. His touch was warm and comforting. Her eyes lifted to his and her stomach flipped.

His voice again took on a deeper, more caring tone. "How's your knee doing?"

"It's fine."

He released her hand. "Why do you keep doing that?" Jacob sat back in the chair and waited for an explanation.

She slid her hands to her lap. "Doing what?"

"Diverting from the truth. Is it a habit with you?" He leaned forward. "Because if it is, you really should know, those mysterious eyes of yours give you away. In fact, I'd say they're down right treasonous."

Ann laughed and shook her head. "Okay, my knee feels foreign to the rest of my leg. Like a softball paired with a golf club."

Jacob smiled at her remark. "At least you still have a sense of humor." He tilted his head to the side and stared at her. Before the lengthened silence became uncomfortable, he added, "You're very pleasant to be around, Annie."

Her breath hitched. *Annie?* No one ever referred to her like that, yet she didn't mind. When it rolled from his tongue, it sounded endearing. *Wait a minute. Endearing? I better slow down.*

Jacob's eyes pooled with desire and Ann knew she needed to put some distance between them. She drew back her legs and to her surprise, Jacob stood and beheld her unashamedly. His eyes trailed her entire body, pausing at intervals. He pulled her in front of him. Her hands were placed on his chest and covered with his own.

"What exactly are your intentions, Mr. Durham?" Her eyes flashed with warning.

His mouth gave way to a hint of a smile. "I think you already have a good idea. But in case you're unsure, let me clear it up for you." His eyes searched hers before falling to her lips. "I intend to kiss you."

His plain and honest statement surprised her and sent her pulse racing.

He returned his gaze to hers. "And to you, I'm Jacob."

As he bent his head toward hers, Ann strained against his hold and stammered. "Wh–where's Mrs. Durham?"

Jacob momentarily closed his eyes and sighed. "After her so-called nervous breakdown, she left us. Two years ago." Her stolen glance at his ring finger caused him to add, "Then she filed for divorce." His voice sounded flat, as though that chapter of his life had been accepted and the memory, now, a nuisance.

She looked up at him and glimpsed a hidden pain not unlike her own. "I'm sorry."

"Hmmm." As though to give thought to his words, Jacob responded, "At the moment, I'm not." He reached out his hand to brush back a tendril of hair from her cheek.

Her eyes weren't the only thing treasonous; her heart thudded in her chest. She shouldn't want this. "Your children . . ." her voice trailed.

"Are asleep," Jacob finished for her as he dropped his hand to her lower back, and pulled her close again.

Her freed hand rested against his bicep. The large, firm bulge of his muscle enticed her. Fighting between what was right and the yearning of her own body, her ability to reason was momentarily stolen as Jacob's mouth closed over hers in a tender kiss. He slowly caressed her lips as though to capture her sweet innocence. His firm mouth became amazingly soft as he took his time exploring the contours of hers.

Her body trembled and Jacob responded by deepening the kiss. His tenderness soon gave way to excitement as he wrapped her closely in his arms. Ann tried to fight against her own reaction, but was too thrilled by the pleasure.

He's a stranger. He's offensive. I don't even know. . . . She gave up. To feel this way in someone's arms was something she'd only dreamed about, and nearly given up on.

Time was lost, as was the passing storm. Thoughts of right and wrong, integrity and honor passed through her mind with barely a flicker of thought.

Jacob continued his hold on her. His warm hand trailed along her spine until Ann gave in. She dissolved all restraint and molded her body to his.

A soft moan of pleasure escaped his lips. Although she felt the same, her growing conviction could no longer be ignored. She struggled against the strong will of desire and drew back as far as he'd allow.

A shuddered breath escaped her. Jacob traced her swollen lips with his thumb seeming to take pride in her breathless emergence. His hand brushed along her jaw to her hair, entwining his fingers in her silken locks.

Ann closed her eyes in hopes to shut out her conscience and allow herself the pleasures Jacob offered. Would it be so wrong? Couldn't she ask forgiveness later? Knowing all too well the right answers, Ann concentrated on scripture she recently read. *"Flee fornication, every sin that a man doeth is without the body; but he that committeth fornication sinneth against his own body."* She opened her eyes and risked losing her confidence at his raw intensity. She had to step away now, knowing that if allowed to escalate, this man wouldn't be able to control himself, and perhaps, she wouldn't want him to.

"Good night, Jacob," she whispered. Now the problem she faced was getting past him to her room. As though in a stare down, they stood facing one another with only the distant rumble of the storm to break the silence.

Jacob's jaw flexed, followed by a deep sigh that sounded more like a low growl. He stepped aside as Ann passed to her room.

She closed the door and sat down on the bed with her knees tucked under her chin. Jacob's touch made her come alive. It was like she'd finally awakened from a deep slumber. How could something like this happen, especially when she was emotionally recovering from being attacked? Was this love or simply an unbelievably, powerful attraction? She wondered what would've happened if she hadn't stepped away. She'd never been tempted to that extent before. The risks that accompanied such lustful acts were never worth it. Especially, the shame she'd feel before God.

She hung her head. Though, her last employer didn't get to accomplish his sinful act, the shame she carried from being a victim was enough. Her stomach tightened just from the thought.

Why didn't she feel that expected fear with Jacob? Past experiences aside, this man was different. She couldn't explain it, but she could sense it. Jacob's demeanor compelled trust. Ann inhaled deeply and relaxed hoping against all odds this was God's will, because never had anyone stirred such feelings inside her.

God, please forgive me for the way I acted. And please help me to have more self-control.

As her thoughts drifted into prayers, Ann rested her head on the pillow and fell into a deep and peaceful sleep until morning.

Chapter Seven

Although a peaceful contentment had settled over the Durham home, hunger created a restless atmosphere outside. The storm passed and left a soft glow of the approaching dawn, which allowed enough light to beckon a hungry doe into the lush pasture. She was high above the creek, just outside the fog's concealment and unaware of her impending danger.

With deliberate furtiveness, the seasoned cougar silently settled its paw before it crouched inches above the ground. Round yellow eyes fixed themselves on the large deer, soon to be its prey.

The doe was no more than fifteen yards away and grazed directly toward the giant cat. The cougar waited. Its tail swished back and forth as the deer edged closer. With muscles tensed, belly and tail dragging the ground, he narrowed the gap. Seven days had passed since he'd killed the calf. Armed with the motivation of hunger, the cougar now turned to larger game.

The doe lifted her head and flicked her ears. She searched for signs of menace and sniffed the air. The wind came from behind, which meant she would never detect the predator that lay in wait. Satisfied of her presumed safety, the lone deer lowered her neck and continued to graze.

Guided by natural instinct, the cougar silently ran toward her and leaped into the air. The frightened doe spun to the side and dug her hooves into the soggy ground, as she desperately tried to out-maneuver the great cat.

He landed on her back and clung with razor-sharp claws. Eyes wide with fear, the doe had little time to panic. The cougar clamped his powerful jaws over her vertebral disk and broke her spinal cord in two.

Her quick death, a tribute to his experienced hunting.

♡♡♡

Jacob got up earlier than usual. He found it useless to lie awake when he could be working. The coffee from last night still sat on the table. He reached for his cup but his eyes lingered on the one last used by Ann. The corners of his mouth tilted upward as he remembered how her body trembled in his arms, how good it felt to hold her. The emotions of indecision had played across her face. He hadn't wanted her to leave, but knew his intentions were wrong. Reluctantly, he'd stepped aside and watched her make her way to the kids' room. His heart swelled to new proportions as his respect for Ann increased.

Along with that, his spirit had begun a battle with his flesh and beckoned him to kneel and ask God for help. *How good it would feel to have that spiritual relationship back.* He'd absorbed the thought before pride returned. He justified his stubbornness because of past hurts and shook off all intentions of prayer. Still a piece of scripture sprang to remembrance, *". . . pride goeth before a fall."*

Again, he cast the thought aside as he walked to the bathroom where he'd laid out clothes so as not to wake his children. Unable to resist the few more steps to Ann's door, he rested a hand on the wooden frame and listened for any sound. Assured she was asleep, and a little disappointed, he opted to forego his shower until after his morning chores, in hopes the lengthened quiet would allow her more rest.

At the door, he slipped on his boots with as little noise as possible and reached for his coat, but instead knocked Ann's to the floor. He stooped to pick it up and noticed its tattered shape. The zipper was stuck in the middle and several teeth were missing. He furrowed his brow. Her hiking boots, he'd noticed last night, were new. He shrugged. How was he supposed to understand women's shopping habits? If she didn't see the need in a new coat, he knew better than to advise her. Though, if she stuck around long enough, he'd have to find her a temporary replacement.

A light mist wet the early morning. The view of the fields hid behind a blanket of low lying fog giving a mysterious presence. Everything was still, as if the whole world slept. The cattle were still bedded down, and even the rooster sat quiet on his perch.

Jacob walked toward the barn, his footsteps muffled by the rain-soaked ground. The path he took was partially finished in slabs of limestone collected from the creek. It had been his and Ethan's fall project and they were both eager to see it finished this summer.

Bordering the path were flower bulbs Emily had chosen and helped plant. Similar to those beside the house, they would come in fuller this spring bringing with them a breath of color. Everything they did to add a feel of happiness would also lead to more security.

Slowly, their broken home would heal.

Trigger emitted a soft nicker as Jacob entered the barn. He raised his head to acknowledge his master then resumed his sleep. Jacob looked at the neatly arranged tack and dusted off the extra saddle. He'd bought it a year earlier. Though it was unusually large, even too big for him, it had proven its use. His children often took turns and rode with him, and because of that, had learned to handle Trigger with ease. Today would be like any other after a big rain, only Ann would have a turn as well.

Ann. Ever since he first laid eyes on her, he couldn't get her out of his mind. And last night–Never had he done anything so rash and unexpected. Not to mention, nearly uncontrolled. If she hadn't pulled back, would he have?

He considered her sleeping in the house with his children. Was she a late sleeper? He hoped not, because his kids definitely weren't. Hearing his dad talk to Candy, Jacob stuck his head out of the barn and exchanged morning waves before Luke entered the house.

Although he often helped out at this early hour, today Luke would also chip in at lunch time. Jacob didn't think Ann possessed a harmful bone in her body, but he still thought it wrong to leave his kids with a stranger, thus prompting him to call on his dad's good nature. Luke seemed happy to oblige his request, almost too willing. Jacob couldn't help but to be suspicious of his dad's motives.

♡♡♡

Ann heard the creak of the front door and sat up in bed. It still looked dark outside but the clock read 5:30 a.m., stating it was morning regardless. As she stretched, her body cried out in complaint for more rest, something she would love to do if only she could. But now that she was awake, curiosity wouldn't let her doze off.

Ann hoped Jacob wouldn't mind if she took a quick shower. She straightened the covers on the bed and changed into her clothes before entering the bathroom. A faded, pink towel and matched washcloth sat on the side of the basin. On top of the cloth lay a plastic sandwich bag, a roll of packaging tape with a pair of small scissors, and a note. Curious, she picked it up. *"Keep your cut dry."* It wasn't signed, but Ann's heart still warmed to the thoughtfulness of its author.

In an effort to make sense of her feelings, she mentally replayed the events of last night. Yes, Jacob was belligerent, rude and headstrong, but something drew her to him. Perhaps it was his social flaws that made his simple acts of kindness that much more meaningful, though it wasn't exactly his kind acts that really moved her. A wry smile stared back at her in the mirror.

Last night had been powerful and it wasn't just the storm. She couldn't remember the last time she'd wanted to be held by a man like that. More often than not, she pushed men away rather than dream of them. Unable to grasp the sense of it all, she bowed her head and asked God for wisdom and direction. Ann knew if there was any hope of reasonable thinking, it would have to come from above.

The smell of sausage greeted her as she exited the bathroom. Did Jacob make breakfast? She stepped into the kitchen, curiosity mingled with hunger. Luke stood at the stove with a towel draped over his shoulder flipping pancakes like a pro. A layer of sausage rested on a paper towel covered plate.

"Good Morning, Sunshine." Luke winked. "Hope you have an appetite this time."

He must have noticed her full dinner plate in the refrigerator. She wouldn't let him down again. "I sure do."

At the unfamiliar sound of her voice, Candy vacated her spot by the stove and hurried to welcome this new stranger. The dog's short little legs moved quickly as she made her way to Ann. A cream colored coat exaggerated the size and intensity of her big brown eyes. Ann was drawn to her immediately. Dogs softened her heart almost as much as children. She knelt down and extended her hand for Candy to sniff.

Luke smiled as Candy bypassed Ann's hand and gave her kisses on the cheek. "I always said that dog was a good judge of character."

Satisfied with the newcomer, Candy took her place at Ann's feet as she sat down at the table. Ann finished the last of the mound of pancakes Luke had given her when Jacob entered.

"Morning, Dad." He turned his attention to where she sat. "Annie."

With his face unshaven and his hair mussed, he boasted an attractive ruggedness. Jacob was definitely one handsome farmer, but something seemed different. His eyes were vacant of any emotion. Ann's stomach knotted. Why did she have to be so foolish? He had probably been caught up in the moment last night and it obviously meant nothing to him. As was typical of a woman, she had given this way too much thought. Disappointment welled in her throat, but she swallowed against it. The best thing to do was pretend she didn't care. But how?

"You must have stuffed her clear full, Dad. She doesn't have room for words."

Ann realized she still stared and hadn't responded to Jacob. "Oh, uh, I—or rather he did. I guess he thought I needed to make up for skipping last night's meal. So watch out, he'll expect the same from you," she teased, thankful for her quick recovery.

Jacob gave a slight smile and excused himself to clean up. Ann glanced at Luke, who waited for her to say something. "What? You're looking at me funny."

"I may be old, but I'm not so old I don't recognize what's going on between you two."

Ann scrunched her brows together. "Then you're more perceptive than I am." Then as if to herself, she mumbled, "He didn't even say two words to me."

Luke leaned on the counter. "He didn't have to and he knows it."

Ann tilted her head to the side and frowned. He walked to the table and patted her hand, sat his coffee cup down and looked directly at Ann. "Love's a funny thing, Hon. It's like your heart's on a roller coaster, especially at the beginning. But if you keep yourself buckled up, the coast in makes it all worthwhile."

Ann couldn't keep her eyes from widening as she stared at Luke.

"It's okay, Sunshine, you both have it." His eyes twinkled.

Speechless, Ann reminded herself to close her mouth.

"I'll leave you to your thoughts." He patted his side. "Come on, Candy. Let's step outside."

Ann's mind reeled from his words. *Why would he assume we're in love? True, I've never known such a rush of feelings for someone before. But to call it love, how ridiculous! Besides, we've just met. For all I know, Jacob might react like this with any woman.*

She realized how pathetic she must be. Twenty-seven years old and never had experienced love, what did that say about her? She had looked for it. Wanted it. Tried to make it happen. But love was elusive, at least for her.

Love. Ann swallowed hard. *Could I really be in love? Surely not. Besides, shouldn't love bring on feelings of happiness and excitement? Not aggravation and confusion.*

She swirled her fork in the remaining syrup on her plate. The lines slowly returned to a murky puddle, just like her thoughts. Dropping the fork in her plate, she carried her dishes to the sink to clean.

"Your hands are never going to heal if you keep getting them soaked."

Ann jumped and grazed herself with a knife she washed. "Ow!"

Jacob reached for her hand and examined her thumb with a deep scowl. "What are you trying to do? You don't have to prove anything by washing dishes. Keep your hands out of the water and let them heal." He grabbed a paper towel and held it against her cut.

What right did he have to tell her what to do? Ann jerked her thumb away. "What makes you think I'm trying to prove anything? I'm keeping myself busy. Surely you don't expect me to sit idle until the creeks go down?"

Jacob softened his voice. "I'll find something for you to do. Just keep your cuts dry."

"Jacob, I'm not a child. My hands aren't even that bad. And besides, it's my body."

He narrowed his eyes and gruffly stated, "Then perhaps we need to remedy that."

Ann stared at him, expecting a further explanation. Instead of an answer, Jacob turned to fill his plate.

Luke stepped inside just as two sets of pattering feet entered the hallway. In unison they called out good morning as they raced to the table, Ethan allowed Emily the satisfaction of winning. Luke grinned along with the children and came over to fill his coffee mug. "Did you two sleep good in the big bed?"

As the conversation began, Ann quietly slipped outside.

I don't understand men. Last night, Jacob acted so different. Now he can hardly stand to look at me. If this is the roller coaster Luke referred to, I want off.

She stomped off in no particular direction, determined to figure out how to get home.

Chapter Eight

Ann, mocked by her thoughts, stomped along a rock path leading to the barn. The man was a stranger, and already she allowed his actions to dictate her emotions. Though she tried to keep her guard up and not be too trustful, every time Jacob came near, all previous thought disappeared.

An animal snorted.

"Oh, good morning, horse. I guess I should pay attention to where I'm going." Ann stepped further inside the barn and followed the equine's beckoning nicker.

"I read once that Indians used to blow on the horse's nose to pass on their scent and make it more at ease. Shall we see if it works?"

The cream colored gelding snorted again and shook his head.

Ann laughed. "I think you got confused, I'm the one supposed to blow. How about we stick to brushing? I bet you'd enjoy that."

♡♡♡

After five minutes of morning chatter, Emily took notice of Ann's disappearance. Her mouth dropped for a moment before she pinched it closed and turned toward her father. With brows drawn, she demanded, "Hey. Where's my Ann?"

Jacob seized the opportunity and rose from the table. "I'll go get her for you."

Ann's coat still hung beside his, so he grabbed them both. He slipped his feet in his boots without tying them and hurried outside.

The soggy ground revealed Ann's tracks leading to the barn. Jacob followed them at a leisurely pace as he pictured her sitting at the table. Her damp hair had been pulled back in a braid and slung over one shoulder. It allowed him full view of her radiant skin, which still glowed from her shower.

Ann was of a rare quality. He had yet to meet a woman like her that could convey humility, grace, and compassion, but still possess enough confidence and spirit to title her as sassy. It was a fun and intriguing combination. When their gazes had locked, his heart slammed against his chest. Flecks of brown and gold danced on top of bright green in excited expectation. Was it too much to hope the sparkle they held was for him? He'd immediately concealed his feelings, for fear he'd make a fool of himself in front of his father. At the risk of ignoring her, he'd made a quick exit.

Before he could rationalize his short outburst in the kitchen, he found himself at the lean-to. He stepped around to the barn and looked inside. Ann had a brush in hand and groomed Trigger while she softly hummed a hymn.

Jacob leaned his shoulder against the entrance and enjoyed the view. "I let him out this morning, and he's already back?"

Ann jumped and spun around. "I didn't realize you were there."

He glanced down at her feet. Her shoes were untied as well. What irony. *She hurried to get away from me, and I rushed to be with her.* He walked to her side and held out the coat so she could slip her arms through. "You must be freezing with that wet hair."

She shrugged slender shoulders and slipped her arms through the sleeves of her tattered coat. "Thanks."

"You left sort of abruptly, you know."

"Well, you weren't exactly welcoming this morning, so I thought it best if I stepped out."

"Sorry about that."

"At least that's a start." Ann's gaze flicked toward Jacob and back to the horse as she ran the brush along its flank.

He frowned and wondered aloud, "A start at what?"

"Aren't you going to apologize for last night, too?"

He grabbed a saddle blanket from the open tack room of the barn and walked back toward Ann, careful to take his time. "I don't make false apologies. And, judging from the way you kissed me back," Jacob gently tugged at her thick braid, "you're not sorry either."

Ann didn't respond. But if her dropped jaw and colored cheeks she turned to hide were any indication, Jacob knew why.

He grasped her elbow and turned her to face him. "Am I right or am I wrong?"

Ann seemed to make a forced effort to meet his gaze. "I'm stuck here until the weather clears, so let's just be level headed about this, okay?"

"So you've changed tactics."

Bewilderment filled her narrow gaze as she jerked her arm from his grasp. "What do you mean by that?"

"Now instead of diverting from the truth, you simply switched topics; clever little maneuver." Jacob referred to her tactic from the night before.

"Stop it! Just stop it."

Not able to control his smile, Jacob asked, "Stop what?"

"Infuriating me!" She stomped her foot. "You—you have this way of getting under my skin and it's maddening."

"Have you ever saddled a horse?"

Ann tilted her head and squinted at Jacob. "What are you talking about?"

Jacob spoke slowly. "Sad-dl-ing a hor-se. Do you know how?"

She blinked rapidly. "No." A firm line replaced her lips.

Jacob swallowed down laughter that threatened to force its way out.

"Now who's switching topics?" She glared.

"Then I'll teach you." Jacob ignored her remark and reached for the brush. He seized Ann's hand and held her small fist in his large palm. Emotion engulfed him. While aggravating her, he allowed himself to forget how easily she could take his breath away. He searched her face and took note of the soft arch of her brows, the thick lashes that outlined her mesmerizing eyes, and the dimples that tried to hide when she wasn't smiling. At last, he rested his gaze on her rose colored lips, savoring the memory of them from last night.

He gently removed the brush from her hand and swallowed. *Take it slow, buddy.* Turning to the horse, he spoke to Ann over his shoulder. "Always start on the horse's left side." After a few brush strokes, he glanced behind him to make sure he still had an audience. Ann's gaze met his. She looked—disappointed? Had she expected a kiss?

Why, he wasn't sure, but he moved to the saddle blankets to continue Ann's short education of horse-care, instead of kissing her. The timing. The timing wasn't right. "Annie, aren't you going to follow me?"

As though jolted from deep thoughts, Ann jumped before she turned to face him. For the second time this morning, he saw color stain her cheeks. He didn't bother to hide his smile. This was too much fun.

Ann diverted her eyes. She left the stall unlatched and strode over to where the saddle and blankets were stored.

"Looks like you have more than one admirer." Jacob nodded at the horse that walked up behind her.

Ann scrunched her brow in question before Trigger lowered his head over her shoulder and pulled her back to his chest in a hug.

She laughed, a joyful noise, and reached up to rub his nose. "And, who would my other admirer be?"

"Emily, of course." Jacob ducked his head to hide his grin. She wanted a direct answer, but he couldn't control the fun of teasing her.

"Humph." Ann turned her full attention to the beige and cream colored gelding. "Why did you name him Trigger?"

While he continued with the tack, Jacob answered, "I'm sure you've heard of Roy Rogers and his horse, Trigger. Well, I figured since mine is a Palomino and just as faithful, it fit."

"What did you call him before he proved his faithfulness?"

"Horse."

She tilted her head to the side and stared at him. Was his logic too hard for her to follow?

Her eyes widened as her focus changed to the tack behind him. "I know you're a strong build Jacob, but surely you don't need a saddle that size?"

Unable to suppress his smirk, Jacob leaned toward Ann. "Taking note of my build, are you? Maybe later you can tell me what other *notes* you're making."

Ann tossed her fist onto her hip and narrowed her gaze. "Don't get over confident. They may not all be positive."

Jacob ignored her humor. "I have this saddle for when the kids ride with me. They can sit in front and hold the reins. That way they learn how to handle Trigger and I'm close by."

"That's considerate."

He quirked an eyebrow. "See, I'm not all brute." He placed his hand on the small of her back and steered her toward the door. "Let's get back to the house. Emily asked for you and I still need to take a look at your knee."

As they walked toward the cabin, he asked, "I'm curious about something. Yesterday you mentioned life's been insulting. Why?"

He noticed her shoulders tense and added, "You don't have to divulge all your secrets at once if you don't want to."

Ann looked up at him with relief in her eyes. "You mean I don't have to tell you what happened in third grade?" She raised her brows in a playful gesture.

"Right." He paused then rubbed the back of his neck. "What *did* happen in third grade?"

Ann laughed. "What fairy tale book have you been reading that says the lady has to tell all to her hero?"

She reached for the door and Jacob covered her hand with his. "So, you're saying I'm your hero?" Ann's eyes darted around. He'd gotten to her. "And I believe the lady in fairy tales is always a princess, right?"

Ann returned her attention to Jacob. Her expression held sweet disbelief. Her lips parted as she stared up at him.

Was her heart pounding as hard as his?

Jacob moved forward and brought his lips close to her ear. "You better be careful, 'cause if you keep looking at me like that, you'll find yourself kissed again."

Ann's sweet exhale lightly brushed against his cheek. He leaned in, their lips so close. Her eyes fluttered closed. His heart began a rapid beat as if it were their first kiss.

"Ann!" Emily swung open the door, tearing the doorknob from Ann's grasp. Jacob wrapped his arms around her and pulled her to him as momentum fought to throw her to the ground.

"I'm afraid this is becoming a habit for us." Ann gave him a thankful smile.

Luke stuck his head around the door from inside. "What's all the commotion about?"

A blush filled Ann's face as she and Luke exchanged glances. She pulled free from Jacob's embrace and cleared her throat. What silent message did his father share with her?

♡♡♡

With the family as an audience in the kitchen when Jacob doctored her cuts, Ann was relieved of his whims of passion, now much to her dismay. The children hovered close by as Jacob removed the gauze. Emily oohed and Ethan thought it would make a cool scar. Aside from her knee being stiff, everything was in good repair. She even agreed to a horse ride after the children had their turns.

When Jacob and Ethan left for the first ride, Ann turned to Emily. "Can I help you with your chores?"

Emily's eyes brightened and she grasped Ann's hand. "Yeah, follow me."

Outside, the weather had cleared and though the clouds still hung low in the sky, the air was momentarily free of moisture. Ann found herself led to the oak-sided chicken house where Emily chattered continually and informed her of the names of each hen and rooster.

"And these new, little chicks are named Princess, Diamond and Diamond."

Ann contained her laugh with effort. "Why did you name two of them with the same name?"

"Because silly, they're twins." She then added in a matter of fact tone and a toss of her head, "They look just alike."

Ann held the basket while Emily gathered the eggs, shooing hens from their nests with comfortable ease. The enthusiastic youth chattered so quickly, bouncing from one subject to the next, Ann could no longer follow the conversation. But when there was a lull in Emily's chatter it brought Ann's gaze to the child. The little bundle of energy stared at her with moist eyes.

"What is it, honey?" Had she failed to answer her? Had Emily felt ignored?

"Ann," her lips formed a pout. "I wish you were my mommy."

Ann's quick intake of breath was followed by a tightening sensation in her chest. It took all she had to keep from crying for the pain that was clearly evident in Emily's eyes. She bit her lip and silently asked God for courage. Was this the devil's way of having fun at her expense? As if opening up an old wound, her heart again longed to hold the little girl she was forced to walk away from. The pain reflected in Emily's eyes was something she saw all too often as a nanny.

"But don't you get to see your mommy?" Ann kneeled down to eye level.

"I don't have one. And I don't talk about it with Daddy, 'cause he gets kinda sad." Emily looked at the ground and scuffed her toe in the dirt.

Ann gently lifted Emily's chin. "How about I pray that God would send you the perfect mom?"

"But He already has. Grandpa and I prayed, and you came." She turned around and yelled, "Beat you to the house." She ran ahead of Ann.

Ann quickly gathered up the eggs that remained and followed after Emily. *God, I don't know what to make of this, so I'll leave it in Your capable hands. But please don't let her heart be broken . . . and please protect mine, too.*

When Ann reentered the house a muffled voice sounded from somewhere near the front room. "Come find me."

Ann smiled with delight. Playing was one of her favorite things about being around children. Lost in a land of make-believe, happiness knew no bounds.

Feigning ignorance, Ann took her time looking under the table and behind the recliner before moving to the couch. Unable to contain her enthusiasm, the little girl exploded with laughter from underneath an afghan and jumped into Ann's arms as she came near.

Emily's soft hands grasped Ann's face and held it in view of her own. "Miss Ann, why are your eyes shiny?"

Ann cleared her throat. "Because playing with you makes me so happy. Now, why don't you tell me where your brush is and I'll work on those tangles."

Emily's interest quickly moved past Ann's teary eyes. "I want my hair braided just like yours."

While Ann combed out Emily's long blonde hair, she warmed to the pleasant chatter of the happy little girl. "Did you know I used to have a rooster named, Peeper?"

Ann smiled as she reached for the ponytail holder Emily held out. "No, I didn't know that. What happened to him?"

"Well first," she huffed and turned to face Ann, who quickly finished securing the braid, "you need to know that all of his feathers grew backwards."

A giggle escaped Ann's lips. "I've never heard of a chicken with backward feathers."

"It is true. They curled up like–hmmm." She tapped a finger to her chin. "Like when Grandpa peels a carrot. Just like that. Anyways, he died. The other chickens didn't like him much. Prob'ly 'cause of his feathers."

"I'm sorry to hear th–," before Ann could finish, Emily grabbed her hand and pulled toward her room.

"Now you can read me a book then I'll let you play hide and seek with me again, only next time you can hide first."

Ann was happy to oblige and humored that she was being *allowed* to play.

Ethan returned from his ride just as Emily began to plot aloud their next adventure. By this time, Ann was grateful for the interruption.

In his best cowboy impersonation, Ethan asked, "Are you ready to ride?"

His sister squealed with excitement as she made for the door. Ann noticed she'd left her coat and came after her as Jacob mentioned it missing. He turned and smiled as she approached.

"See you for lunch." Ann waved as she backed toward the house.

♡♡♡

Jacob helped Emily onto Trigger before he mounted behind her. As they rode off he turned to look back. Ann still stood near the cabin watching. He snapped a mental photo. That was a sight he wanted to hold on to.

Not one to be quiet, Emily stole her dad's attention as she relayed all she and Ann did together. But what really caught his interest was what she told him next. "She also told me she likes you!"

"What? She said that, huh?" Jacob pondered her statement before saying, more to himself than Emily, "I wonder why she said that?"

"Because I asked her, silly," Emily giggled. "And then I asked her if she liked you a lot and she said, yes!" Emily triumphantly explained.

Jacob began to understand. He hoped Ann did like him, but from the sounds of things, Emily all but said the words for her. "Can you tell me what else you two talked about?"

"She used to be a babysitter for a girl named, Amy. She said she was the kind of babysitter that lived with Amy; I forgot what she called it. But I'm older than that

72

girl." The latter was spoken with pride. "I think Ann should live with us, Daddy. She could be my babysitter."

"But you don't need a babysitter, honey, you have Grandpa and me."

"But I need Ann, and she says she really likes kids and I'm a kid, so that's why she needs to live with us." She whined her last words.

Jacob smiled at his daughter's youthful logic. He could definitely get used to the idea of having Ann around. But before his heart could warm to the idea of a future with her, memories of the past shadowed his happiness.

Why should he even try? He obviously lacked what it took to keep a woman content, or else he'd still be married.

Chapter Nine

Ann watched Jacob and his daughter until they disappeared over the hill. Bubbly sensations tickled inside and tempted her to twirl around with her arms in the air. She laughed at the idea and went inside to straighten up the mess she and Emily made. What a wonderful day this turned out to be. But what happens after this? She'd never thought about that. Living in the moment was fun, but it would eventually come to an end. And what then?

When finished cleaning up the mess, she turned to take a closer look at the Durham home. It was bigger than she first imagined. Shaped like a "T," the kitchen entrance opened from the back and joined the living room. A hallway led to two bedrooms and created the top of the "T."

She turned her attention to the living room and stood with hands on her hips; perhaps it held answers to Jacob's past. He'd had a wife. Where was she, had she died? Had they been happy together?

Surely they had family photos. The room was furnished with an older sofa and recliner on a hardwood floor. She opened the cabinet door on a small side table. A box hid under a pile of old magazines and coloring books. Her eyes darted toward the door. How long had it been since Jacob and Emily rode off?

Curiosity beckoned her to throw caution to the wind and open the lid. She lifted it an inch and peeked inside. Unable to see, she took a breath of courage and tossed the lid to the side.

Crayons.

Disappointment settled in her chest. What had she expected? Repositioning the box the way she found it, she stood and looked around the room.

A framed print decorated the wall adjacent of the door. A wintry scene displayed a row of saddled horses with two civil war soldiers making their rounds on foot. Ann was familiar with the artist and knew something significant hid in the picture, often in the opposite direction her work naturally led the viewer's eyes. Ann searched the painting and spotted two Indians that snuck by unseen.

Perhaps I'm a bit like those Indians. The image didn't set well. With a defeated sigh, she plopped into the recliner.

Aha. On top of an end table sat a framed family photo. It looked to be roughly a year old with the children, their Grandpa Luke and most likely, his wife. Ann peered at the woman. A pang of regret swept through her for not having met her. Emily had mentioned she'd passed on. Even through the picture, it appeared the woman possessed a Godly wisdom Ann would've benefited from knowing. In the background stood a steeple from a church. It comforted her to think perhaps they attended church on a regular basis.

Since she already saw the rest of the house, and nothing caught her attention, she ended her search. Nosiness wasn't her style. At least she had the comfort of the church in the background of the picture. Refocused, she started cleaning.

Though the house wasn't cluttered, it lacked a woman's touch. She trailed her finger across the window seal and noted the layer of dust. A quick search beneath the kitchen sink rewarded her with a can of dusting spray. The chore didn't last long enough to still her nerves.

Ann left the clean lemon scent that now filtered through the house and stepped outside. Her shoulders drooped with disappointment. They still hadn't returned. She sighed and hoped a walk would help control the jitters that continued to build the longer he was gone. Jonquills had already bloomed alongside the house. Many other flowers were leafed out, but without their blooms, she couldn't identify them. She rounded the corner and saw Luke and Ethan outside. Without hesitation, she followed their beckoning waves to join them and crossed the gravel road.

Ethan grabbed her hand and pulled her inside his grandparent's home. He proudly gave her a tour as his grandpa smiled fondly and followed behind.

Luke's home held an old-fashioned appeal. Everything was dated, just like it should be. In the main room, faded wall paper hung behind numerous portraits of their small family.

"You'll love the upstairs, Ann. You're short enough you won't even hit your head on the ceilings." Ethan bounded up the creaky stairs that led to two small bedrooms with shortened ceilings.

After their descent, Ann found her favorite room to be the kitchen. An old chrome table and chair set, reminiscent of another era, centered the worn yellow linoleum. Luke opened a painted, plywood cabinet door to retrieve a few glasses.

"You want some tea?" He filled the glasses while Ann and Ethan took their seats at the table. "This old house has been around far longer than I have."

He eyed Ann carefully. "You know, most young couples nowadays wouldn't dare settle for a place like this. They want all that new and fancy stuff." He waved a hand at his out-dated cabinets.

Ann's gaze followed Luke's hand before she allowed it to settle back on him. "I'm sure you're right. But I wouldn't be included in that group. I've lived in some fancy places and they not only lack the charm that your home affords, they also lack the contentment I feel here. And, it makes sense. When families have high, unnecessary mortgages to meet each month, it takes away from the enjoyment of the home."

Luke sat back in his chair as though satisfied. Had she correctly answered something that bothered him? He continued the conversation, centering on the life of a farmer. If Ann didn't know better, Luke was preparing her for what would be expected should she ever find herself as a farmer's wife. She wasn't offended by his efforts. She was honored he wanted to prepare her, instead of scare her off. His stories were both honest and amusing, and kept her and Ethan laughing whole heartedly.

"One of my favorite stories was when Christine, that was my wife's name, and I were brush-hogging the field. It was before Jacob was born. I guess we'd been married almost a year. We were seated on the tractor together and scared up a batch of baby skunks. Now, if you'd known Christine, you'd know that lady couldn't turn her back on any of God's creatures. Naturally, she wanted to catch them so they weren't left defenseless without any cover. Through some fast talking, she convinced me babies couldn't spray.

"I should've known better, but being so in love with that woman, I chose to believe her. So, I shut down the tractor and we commenced to chasing those little, striped critters around. We finally got one cornered together, and just as Christine reached to pick it up, it turned its baby tail up and, oh well, you can guess the rest of the story." Luke chuckled. "Someone from the community would stop by with canned tomato juice each day for the next week!"

"And that's why they always canned extra tomatoes each year." Jacob's voice surprised them as he stepped into the kitchen. Emily bounded onto Ann's lap and embraced her in a big hug.

"Hi, we didn't hear you come in." Ann returned Emily's hug, taking in the sweet scent of the outdoors that clung to her hair.

Jacob's gaze remained glued to Ann as she held Emily. "I thought we'd get a bite to eat then you can join me when I meet the neighbors."

Luke scooted back his chair and went to the refrigerator. "In that case, let's have sandwiches while we're all here."

Over lunch, Emily filled them in about the new calves, how she named each one, and what their names were. Ann stole a look at Ethan to see if he would argue to her naming all of them, but was surprised to see him laugh at Emily's selfish antics and pass it off with a simple shake of his head. He appeared far more mature than she earlier guessed, even to the point of understanding his sister's youthful age and leaving the unimportant battles alone. Emily would probably never have to resort to climbing trees to be a part of her brother's life. Suddenly protective, Ann was glad. She cringed at the thought of Emily high in a tree then almost laughed out loud. She sounded just like her mother.

With lunch over, Luke and the children sat down to watch an old western. Though there wasn't an antenna, he maintained a television and VCR to enjoy movies. As they settled in, Jacob took the opportunity to guide Ann outside for the promised ride.

The refreshing weather nipped at her cheeks. Although it was still March, she could sense spring edging in closer, but even that wasn't enough comfort to hold her attention. As the door closed behind Jacob, she realized how relaxed she *had* been. Now that they were alone again, her tangled nerves returned to the familiar jittery sensation. Being alone with Jacob brought about feelings of anticipation along with apprehension. She was excited to be with him, but worried if he was feeling the same or not. Though his past actions should be enough to clear away her doubts, she still succumbed to nagging worry.

In hopes of easing her spirit, she turned to make small talk, but caught Jacob admiring her. Her mouth parted in surprise before she closed it and gave him a sheepish smile. He reached for her hand and held it as they walked back to the cabin. His touch held a welcomed sweet calm.

Ann spied Jacob's horse, ready to ride again, tethered near an oak tree. "Where's the other horse?"

Jacob helped her mount up, careful of her knee. "Trigger's all I've got." Then he quickly mounted behind her.

Ann stiffened at his nearness, his legs nestled into the bend of her own. Sharing a saddle together wasn't what she had in mind, though it was becoming clear it was exactly what Jacob had intended.

"Relax," he whispered in her ear, "I *can* be a gentleman."

"I'm sure you can. I'm just not convinced you *will*."

He laughed but withheld any response. With his left hand resting on his leg, he reached around Ann with his right and retrieved the reins. He encouraged Trigger along, and they headed toward the creek to check in with his neighbors.

Ann inhaled deeply and tried to hold it. Though after a moment she realized it was futile to fight against the joy that rose within her. Earlier, Jacob had more or less called her a princess. Now, it seemed as though the fairytale would continue, while she rode away with her prince.

Jacob's voice interrupted her thoughts. "I stopped inside the house before going over to Dad's. Thank you for cleaning up the place. It looks great."

Ann raised her brows in surprise, not only because Jacob noticed, but that he also thanked her. Even as wonderful as her own father was, rarely did he thank her mother for all her efforts. She looked at him over her shoulder. "You're welcome. It helped pass the time."

Then she held her palms up so he could see. "I didn't even get my hands wet."

Jacob seized the opportunity to touch her again and took one of her hands in his. "Good, they're looking much better." He pulled her hand to his lips and planted a soft kiss over her cut before gently placing it back on the saddle horn.

♡♡♡

Jacob considered their developing relationship as they rode quietly through the field. He'd made the decision to avoid getting too close to Ann in conversation and in the physical sense. The more she opened up, the more entangled his heart became with hers. Since he'd never experienced such a connection with someone before, he feared losing control.

Now, however, he had to admit what an improbability his idea posed, especially since they shared the same saddle. A fact he'd refused to consider when he made his hapless plan. His only hope was that her strength would be enough for both of them.

Ann shifted in the saddle before she spoke. "I know the Stevenson's a little. When you first mentioned them, the name sounded familiar but it didn't occur to me who they were until today."

Curious, he asked, "How's that? They don't usually socialize with many people."

"They stopped by one day when I was working outside so we got to talking, and Mrs. Stevenson asked me over for the next day. I have to warn you though, I didn't impress her."

"If you were wearing those jeans and a little shirt, I can see why not." He laughed.

"Actually, I tried to be respectful. I dressed in one of Uncle Frank's sweatshirts. I suppose I could have worn one of my dresses, but I doubt they'd approve of the lengths."

"Maybe I should see you in them and give you my opinion."

"Ha, ha." She began to twirl a strand of hair.

"Seriously," he asked as he fought against the vision of Ann in a short skirt, "why weren't they impressed?"

"They tried to convert me to their convictions, but I wasn't very moldable."

Jacob let out a hearty laugh to which Ann replied, "I'm glad you find this so funny. At my expense, I might add. You realize they probably think I'm bound for hell."

"Look at it this way; you didn't waste any time getting to know what they're like, so be thankful." Jacob paused. "By the way, Mrs. Stevenson home-schools my children."

Ann turned as much as the saddle would allow and faced him. "What? Why and how do you measure up to their standards?"

The sun's light drew on the color of her freckles and challenged him to drop their conversation and kiss each little brown speck. He drew his attention to her eyes; he loved the way the green brightened as they grew wide with aggravation. He touched a hand to her soft cheek and smiled. "Don't get so riled. They're merely helping out a single father, who they probably see as despondent, in hopes of raising his children to their way of thinking."

Ann gaped. "And that's okay with you?"

"Annie, I talk with my children every evening over what they've been taught. The Stevenson's are a bit old fashioned with their convictions, but that's *their* convictions, not mine. And I don't think they mean any harm. Besides, in my opinion, my kids are much safer in their hands than public schools."

Ann turned back around, her posture more relaxed. "I guess the Stevenson's aren't wrong in their way of life. They choose to live more restricted because that's how they're convicted. The thing I didn't like was feeling judged by them. But I suppose even that isn't a reflection of their way of life. I've met other families of similar beliefs and enjoyed my time with them. The Stevenson's were at odds with me from the start. Why they ever invited me over is a mystery to me."

She paused before she asked, "Do you think God convicts everyone differently?"

Jacob considered her question. "To some extent, yes. I think you see examples of that in the Bible if you read about Paul and his thoughts of some of the other disciples."

"That's how I see it, too. But I don't think your neighbors do."

"You mean the ones standing over there?" Jacob pointed to the rigid outlines of his neighbors.

Mr. Stevenson stood across the overflowing creek with two of his sons. He emitted a foreboding presence that seemed centered on Ann.

Chapter Ten

Mr. Stevenson cupped his hand around his mouth and shouted from across the creek. "Good afternoon, Jacob. How are the children?"

Ann cringed from his voice. He was a stern man that, for an unexplainable reason, made her want to disappear.

Jacob slid down from his mount. "Fine. Excited about storms and no school." He walked closer to the bank with Trigger's reins in his hand.

"Yes, it's a shame they'll miss out on a few days." Mr. Stevenson wasn't one prone to jester. He took school as seriously as every other part of life.

He turned his attention toward Ann, and shouted to be heard over the roar of the creek. "Who might your friend be?"

Still sitting atop Trigger, she could only hope he had a bad memory.

Jacob's chest swelled. "This here's Ms. Annie McHaven."

Even from the distance the creek put between them, Ann could see Mr. Stevenson's brow furrow as he rubbed his thumb across the side of his index finger in an agitated fashion. Had he noted the endearing way

Jacob referred to her? She needed to break the growing silence. Ann planted a smile on her face and waved. "Good morning, Mr. Stevenson!"

As though she hadn't even spoken, he directed his speech back to Jacob. "Have you enough food for the children? We're supposed to get another bucket of rain tonight."

"Yes, thank you, though I could use a favor. Since Annie's going to be stuck here until the creeks go down, could you call Mr. Whitener and let him know she's here. He'll probably be checking in on her and we don't want him to worry."

Ann knew her reputation was shot. Not only did Jacob refer to her as Annie, something no one else did, he used the word "we," as if they made decisions together. *But we did. We made the decision about Mr. Whitener together.* Jacob also asked her to ride with him, he didn't command it. Maybe there was hope for this man after all, and why did that thought leave her so happy?

The sound of Mr. Stevenson's voice brought her out of her reflections.

"I will for you, Jacob. Will that be all?" he asked, in blatant dismissal.

"Just one more thing I want you to be aware of. I've found prints of a big cat. I think it's getting my calves. Be careful."

"Thank you, Jacob." Mr. Stevenson steered his sons back in the direction of their house.

"How could you tell they were cat prints and not a dog's?" Ann couldn't tell one print from another. Of course, the suburbs didn't offer any reason for that type of knowledge.

"You know a cat has retractable claws, right?"

She nodded.

"A cat only extracts them when needed, so when it's running or walking you can't see the claw marks. But dogs can't retract their claws, so theirs show up. And since a cougar's foot is huge, its track isn't something you could confuse with a house cat or even a bobcat."

He rubbed his chin. What was he thinking? "I planned to show the ones I found to Ethan so he would know what to be aware of, but the rain took care of that."

"Do you think Mr. Stevenson believed you?" Ann asked.

"I don't know." Jacob stroked Trigger's neck. "No one around here wants to, but he should be cautious, especially since he has so many young ones. Seven children still live at home. That's a lot to keep up with."

"Wow, and I always thought four would be a lot." She spoke aloud without considering her audience. She could feel Jacob's eyes on her and looked down from on top of Trigger.

His mouth twitched into a crooked grin. "Four, huh? Is that how many kids you want?"

Redness probably matched the warmth in her cheeks. How does he keep doing this?

"Did you grow up in a large family?"

Her shoulders relaxed before she answered, thankful for the change of direction. "There were twelve cousins, and we were all similar in age. My dad has three brothers and two sisters, so family get-togethers were always fun and loud. My brother and I were never short on playmates."

"It must have been nice to grow up with so many people you could trust."

Ann smiled and looked off in the distance as the warmth washed away from her cheeks. Flashbacks of playing with her cousins and the loud ring of laughter from adults gathered together rang in her mind.

"I guess that's probably why you wanted four children, so they could experience a life like yours."

"I guess." The pleasant feeling her memories had wrought quickly faded as she realized what he'd done. She groaned. "Happy? You got your answer."

"Yep." Jacob mounted behind Ann and gave Trigger an encouraging nudge of his heels.

Ann tried not to dwell on Jacob's curiosity but couldn't help herself. Would he be willing to add to his children? Did God have a family planned for her all along? She pushed the thoughts from her mind. Jacob sat too close for her to think about that now. She focused her attention back to their ride.

The creek had swelled well past its banks and made a small river through the property. Native Black Willows that usually hung in a quiet and serene manner along the water's edge, now found themselves likened unto Cypress. A great blue heron, spooked by their presence, mounted up on giant wings and took flight.

"This is simply beautiful. I've always thought of spring as the annual rebirth of creation. Being in the midst of the country only confirms it."

"Do you think it would ever bore you?"

"Oh no, I've always wanted to live in the country. By the way, where are we headed?"

"I figured you might enjoy seeing more of the property. Especially if we get more rain, I'd hate for you to feel cooped up in the house."

"Oh, I wouldn't. Your children are too delightful and your home is so cozy. Like the kind of place where you want to get snowed in." Ann imagined snow drifting around the cabin while a fire blazed away in the hearth.

Jacob lean forward, his breath whispered against her ear. "Am I the kind of man you could picture being snowed in with?"

Jacob's directness stunned Ann, and at the same time, excited her. *Things like this don't happen this fast. Who falls in love this early in a relationship? And, why would Jacob want me? Does he think I could be a good enough mother for his children? I've just learned his last name, but I don't know anything of his past. What happened to his wife and what kind of husband had he been?* She tried to slow things down while she still had the will.

Her throat tightened but she forced her voice to respond. "Jacob, I've had some bad experiences and I'm not ready for—for—" she let her voice drift as her mind tried to remember what exactly she didn't want.

"Look, Ann," Jacob reined Trigger to a stop and dismounted. His warm hands cupped her waist and pulled her down beside him. "If it's me you have a problem with, you need to say it. But if this is something from the past, then you'll just have to move forward, 'cause I'm not backing down."

Ann trembled from the truth and confidence of Jacob's words. Unaware of how to respond, she allowed him to continue.

"There's a longing inside you that wants to trust, to feel secure in someone's arms." He pulled her to him. "Trust in me, Annie. Let my arms be the ones to hold you." He brought his lips to hers and kissed her. His mouth beckoned for a response as the tenderness faded and something more driven took its place.

Ann remembered Luke's words, "You couldn't be in better hands." She relaxed in Jacob's embrace and returned his kiss. She welcomed the familiar, languid warmth that filled her limbs and left her in want of more.

As Jacob slid his coarse hand against the back of her neck to draw her closer, a cool breeze interrupted the moment. He exhaled a deep sigh and stepped back. "You're something special, Annie."

Ann couldn't speak for fear the water brimming in her eyes would turn to tears. Her heart ached for him. Her lips still tingled from the touch of his. She wanted so much to be back in his arms. Was it time to let go of the past?

An ugly guilt manifested itself in her mind. What about the rumors her employers had spread? If word reached Jacob, would he find enough fault in her to believe them?

Jacob accepted her silence and placed a tender kiss on her forehead. "Let's head back before it gets too late."

♡♡♡

The wind stirred around them as they rode on in silence. Jacob inhaled Ann's natural sweetness mixed with soap from the morning's shower and pictured her as his wife. He could see them in a family photo with his two children happily smiling, a toddler in his arms and Ann's belly swollen with their fourth. Everything she said and did caused Jacob to desire her more. The tender nurturing she showed his children. The instant camaraderie she shared with his dad. The way her eyes lit up whenever she caught him staring.

If the rain washed out the bridge, her stay would be lengthened.

Let it rain.

They'd only covered a short distance before Trigger snorted and tossed his head. He nervously backed up. Ann tightened her hold on the saddle horn while Jacob reached around with his other hand to grab one of the reins. He could feel the horse tremble beneath them and knew it wanted to bolt. He tightened his thighs around the horse' sides and pulled one rein to his hip, which forced Trigger in circles until he calmed. With a glance ahead, he spotted the cause of the upset. Beside the rain soaked field, partially hidden under a low-lying branch, lay a fresh kill. A doe.

"Ooh! What in the world–?" Ann clasped a hand over her mouth.

The metallic smell of blood tainted the air. Jacob soothed Trigger's nerves. "It's okay, boy. You did good. You did good, all right." He waited to answer Ann until he scanned the trees and underbrush for any sign of the lion.

"That was a doe. A pretty good sized one, too. A cougar brought it down, probably early this morning."

"How can you tell?"

"Look at its wounds. A lion opens up the chest and eats the heart, lungs and other soft organs first. Since it's partly covered, I imagine it got full for now. But I suspect it's not far off. We'd better get back to the house."

"You said lion. Now I'm confused. Is there a cougar and a lion we're looking for?"

Jacob directed Trigger away from the kill before. "No, they're all the same thing. It depends on where you're from, whether you refer to it as a mountain lion, puma, panther, or cougar."

"How do you know all this?"

"We've always had them around. As a kid, their stories fascinated me, so I did my own research."

Jacob continued to make conversation in an effort to steer Ann's thoughts away from their find. "I recently bought a Sharps 45-70 at a sale. Now I'll be able to justify its expense."

"What's that?"

"A 45-70 is the rifle I've always dreamed of owning. It represents the Wild West," he deepened his voice playfully, "where men were men."

Ann turned to look back at Jacob and smiled. "So, do you have chaps and a cowboy hat to go with it?"

Jacob was pleased with the result of their conversation. Ann's mind was now refocused. "Don't forget my spurs."

Her laughter was followed by a flash of lightning.

Jacob looked across the sky. "If I can beat the storm, I might have a chance to use it."

Ann clutched Jacob's arm. "You're not coming after it by yourself, are you?"

He leaned over her shoulder and whispered in her ear, "Why Miss Annie," he drawled, "would that be concern in your voice?"

Trigger was more willing to answer than Ann. The horse stretched out his legs and pulled for more rein as he bolted toward home. Jacob held Ann safely against his chest and let him run. The lightning flashed repeatedly as they raced for the safety of the barn.

Chapter Eleven

The sun rested on the horizon by the time Jacob and Ann returned to the barn. Luke and Ethan ran out to meet them. Ethan paused for breath. "What's going on, Dad?"

Luke mentioned Ann's ghostly pallor and helped her down while Jacob relayed their findings.

"We found a doe carcass in the back field. I bet that cougar brought it down sometime this morning, which means it'll be back. I might be able to snag it if I hurry."

"Wow, can I go with you? You'll need an extra set of eyes, Dad." Ethan straightened his eight year old frame to its full height, apparently wanting to be seen as capable as he must feel.

"Son, I appreciate that, but I couldn't live with myself if something went wrong. These cats don't leave any room for mistakes." Jacob missed the immediate slump in his son's shoulders and looked at the sky through the barn door. "It looks like I'm going to miss my chance anyway. From the size and color of those thunder clouds, I'd no sooner get out there than be caught in a down pour."

A clap of thunder resounded throughout the sky as the wind picked up speed.

"Let's not waste any time getting Trigger wiped down." Luke grabbed a towel to dry off the sweat-soaked gelding.

"You're welcome to stay with us, Dad, 'til this storm passes by. Bring Candy over if you like."

"Thanks for the offer, Son. Maybe next time." Luke finished wiping down the nervous animal before he said good night. He patted Ann's arm as he went out.

"Why doesn't he ever stay?" asked Ann.

"He helps out a lot, but I think he still needs his personal space." Jacob looked toward the house as lightning streaked across the sky. "We'd better get inside before Emily wakes up from her nap."

♡♡♡

Ann hung up their coats while Jacob tried to comfort Emily. She jumped from a clap of thunder and knocked all the coats down again. The storm rolled in with more intensity than the night before. Lightning lit up the sky from every direction. No wonder the child was scared.

Jacob held his crying daughter and patted her back as she soaked his shirt in tears. "Emily, you have to stop crying. We were right outside, you were safe, and we were coming in." He heaved a sigh and turned to Ann. "Maybe you could sing to her again. I'm at a loss here."

"Sure." Ann doubted she could comfort the distraught little girl any more than her father, but would try.

Beside the fire place in a wooden, rocking chair, Ann rocked and sang as Ethan helped build a fire with his dad. She wrapped a quilt around Emily's small frame and the girl nestled as close as she could, as though to savor the offered security. The soft crackle of the fire created a peaceful calm that filtered throughout the room.

As the night wore on, the horror of finding the dead deer faded. Ann relaxed and enjoyed being part of a family. No longer wanting to warn off her growing feelings, she allowed herself a moment to contemplate Jacob's earlier statement. Does he really mean it? If he isn't going to back down, could this mean–Unwilling to finish her thought, she secretly hoped he would bring it up again. She stole a look in his direction. Her eyes only confirmed what her heart already claimed.

Jacob instructed Ethan how to lay the blankets where they could sleep in front of the fireplace so the children wouldn't be afraid of the storm. Ann watched an ornery smile capture Ethan's lips. He grabbed a pillow and swung it at his dad. Jacob laughed and returned fire with fire.

Emily sat up on Ann's lap and clapped her hands. "Get 'im, Daddy."

Laughter filled the house as Jacob and Ethan continued to entertain the girls, disrupting the blankets they'd so carefully laid out. Ethan swung again and connected with Jacob's head.

"That was rough. You better watch yourself."

His words were lost on Ethan who was caught in a fit of laughter. Everyone laughed with him until Jacob's swing connected with the corner of the side table. Feathers burst into the air and scattered around the room onto its occupants. For one small moment, the room became silent with disbelief. How would Jacob handle the mess? He looked over at Ethan. A joyful noise erupted from deep inside him and soon they were all near tears with laughter.

Jacob's eyes caught Ann's and held them with a deep affection. Ann wanted to hold on to the joy they radiated. She admired him in his state of upheaval. His hair was tousled, despite his attempt to comb it with his fingers. A lock continued to tease his eyes. His plaid shirt was partially untucked from his jeans, which only added to his appeal. He looked so relaxed, so happy.

Jacob walked over to her on his way to his room and waited as the children ran past to gather their stuffed toys and another pillow. "I'm glad you're here, Annie."

Just as she opened her mouth to respond the children returned.

Ethan shouted, "Come on Annie, we have a book to read."

Even their interruptions were welcomed. Watching them open up to her so readily helped comfort the constant yearning for children of her own; which is what made walking away from her chosen profession as a nanny so difficult. It had been a tough decision, and though she still wasn't sure what direction God would send her, that door was undoubtedly closed.

After three books, they roasted marshmallows over the fire in the living room. Jacob wiped the children's sticky fingers before he skewered the hotdogs.

"Do you always eat dessert before dinner?" Ann couldn't help her curiosity.

Emily giggled. "No, silly."

"Only when we eat hotdogs. Right kids?"

"Yes," they shouted in unison.

Family traditions. They were important. Usually a mother provided those special occasions. Instead, Ann watched Jacob skewer another marshmallow for Emily.

"You're awfully quiet, Annie," Jacob's baritone voice rumbled.

Ann ducked her head and smiled. "Oh, I was just thinking." She cleared her throat. "If you didn't have any siblings, Jacob, and you lived all the way out here, what did you do for fun?"

"I had school and my folks. You might have noticed with Dad, they were up in their years before I finally came along. I helped them out a lot. And when we didn't work, there was always plenty of hunting and fishing." He smiled at his last statement. "I remember setting trout-lines with my dad when I was about six."

Ann frowned. "Trout-lines?"

"Oh yeah, we have a city girl in our midst." The children giggled at their father's remark. "A trout-line is a long cord with a weight at the end. In the middle are several leads of rope with baited hooks. You toss the weighted end of the rope into the creek and secure the remaining end to a tree." He acknowledged Ann's understanding before he continued. "We got up with the sun the next morning to check 'em before any caught fish wiggled loose. My dad pulled the first line. On one of the hooks flapped the biggest catfish I'd ever seen at the time, but that was nothing compared to what was on my line."

The children leaned in closer, waiting for Jacob to release them from suspense.

"My line was so heavy I called out to Dad to help me with it. We pulled and pulled and then something big started thrashing at the water's surface. I was scared and wanted to run, but Dad was behind me so all I could do was brace myself for the worst. As we pulled, what looked like a prehistoric monster flipped out of the water and jerked himself loose of the hook."

"What was it, Dad?" Ethan's eyes grew wide with excitement. Jacob possessed the same amount of skill at story telling as his father and was easily rewarded with their apt attention.

"A gar. An alligator gar to be exact. It's a fish. They have long skinny snouts lined with lots and lots of sharp teeth. They're really harmless, but at five feet long, harmless was the last thing I was thinking."

Once again, Ann found her feelings deepen for this man. He had so many of the qualities that she had once labeled nonexistent in a single human being. She prayed again for this to be God's will for her life. Please, please, please!

♡♡♡

Ann watched Jacob stare into the fire for a long while. Where were his thoughts taking him? "They're asleep," she whispered.

He didn't turn his gaze right away, and when he did, he gave his full attention to the two children and made sure they were covered before he looked at her.

"What exactly were you doing before you came here?" His question came out of nowhere.

He lay stretched out in front of the fire with Ann across from him and the children fast asleep on the pile of blankets.

Ann scooted from the chair to sit beside him on the floor. She drew her knees to her chest and exhaled. *Where do I start?* Before she could hesitate further, the words tumbled out of her mouth.

"I was a nanny for a high-society couple up north. An ideal job, or so, I thought. Amy was their three-year-old daughter, and after I came they added a baby boy to the picture. Things went from good, to kind of decent, to unbearable. The couple fought all the time. The husband started to drink more and more.

"So that's why you left?"

Ann twirled a strand of hair. "Not, exactly." She chewed her lip with indecision. Tell him. Not tell him. She stole a quick glance at Jacob. All she needed to continue was revealed in the depth of his eyes. Concern. Patience. Protection.

"Umm . . . I wound up losing my job, and because of rumors, I couldn't find other employment." Ann batted her lashes against the threat of tears. Why was this so difficult to tell? She wasn't the guilty party.

"My employer forced his way into my room one night," she swallowed the rising lump in her throat and turned her face away.

Beside her, Jacob straightened. He balled his hands into fists as a muscle in his jaw twitched.

The tip of Ann's finger turned white from the tightness of the wound hair. "His wife happened to walk by and she got him . . . he didn't get to . . . I, I wasn't hurt."

Jacob took hold of her hand. "Come here," he said as he pulled her next to him. He wrapped his arm around her shoulders in a protective gesture and rested his head against hers. "You're safe now."

Tears still threatened to flow. She may be safe, but how could she move past the guilt? Ann's posture remained stiff beside Jacob.

As if sensing her discomfort, he released her and tilted her chin to meet his eyes. "What else?"

Ann's lips quivered. Shame forced her eyes to the floor. "They said some really nasty things about me after I was fired. I know they're not true, but I still feel guilty." Her voice cracked at the omission. "If I would have left earlier . . ."

"That's no reason to feel guilty, Annie."

"You don't understand. I knew things weren't right."

The nine month old child had gotten her out of bed for a bottle of milk. While wrestling with him in the kitchen, her robe came undone. Her employer watched the scene from the shadows of another room. When she realized he was there, she hurriedly retreated to her bedroom and shut the door.

Still, there were other times she heard her name included in their arguments. Her presence was becoming a source of discomfort. A wedge formed between her employers. The children's parents. Yet, because of her own selfish attachment to the children, she'd stayed.

Ann stared at the red and orange flames as they danced in the hearth. "I've asked God to forgive me, because I know where I was to blame. But I can't seem to move past what they said or what he did. It's like a continual rerun being played in my mind."

Jacob shifted on the floor. "Ann, the only power their words and his actions have is the power you give them. You're allowing them to have this control over you."

Ann turned to face him, frustration colored her cheeks. "But you—I—"

"Ann." Jacob grasped her shoulders. "You're strong and capable. Take back the reins."

Could it be that simple? Have I been feeding this myself? Ann turned back to the fire and watched it laugh at her weakness. All it would take to tame that flame is a bucket of water. She stared at Jacob with admiration. He was right. She'd stop feeding the fire.

Jacob's words were a comfort to her soul. She never planned to tell him, but found it to be a huge release.

The tension she'd carried since the incident, slowly faded. She rested her head against his broad shoulder and relished the offered safe-haven. His arm came around her and pulled her tight before he whispered, "Glad you figured it out."

Someone had once described love as a feeling of not being able to see your life without that person. She hadn't been able to fully grasp that idea, until now.

♡♡♡

Ann stirred from beneath a blanket and tried to turn over but couldn't. Sandwiched between Ethan and Emily, they'd rolled on each side of her quilt. The fire began to crackle, sending sparks shooting upward in the hearth. The smell of warmth and wood tickled her senses. She stretched her legs and peered over her feet. Jacob had one knee on the floor while his forearm rested on the other. His white t-shirt stretched tight against his muscular back as he positioned each log in place.

"Psst," she whispered, "can you help me escape?"

Jacob looked over his shoulder and rubbed his chin thoughtfully. "Looks like they have you pinned."

"Yeah, I know." Unable to move her arms Ann blew at the curl of hair tickling her nose. "So are you going to help me?"

Jacob's smile looked devious. "Sure."

He turned his body to face her while still on his knees. With a hand around each ankle, he pulled her toward him and drug Ann underneath the blanket.

She laughed quietly when her head was finally exposed and accepted Jacob's hands as he pulled her to a sitting position.

"I wouldn't have done it that way, but I guess it worked." She still wore a smile as she smoothed back her hair.

Jacob's eyes gleamed. "You're even beautiful when you're asleep."

Stunned, all Ann could do was look up at him. No one had ever told her she was beautiful; cute, yes, even pretty a few times, but never beautiful.

Jacob gently lifted her left hand and rubbed her empty ring finger. "What will I do with myself when you're gone, Annie?"

Her heart felt as if it would burst. She held her breath, wanting the moment to last. "Come and get me to sing to Emily when it storms."

"In that case, I'll be hoping for lots of thunder." His voice was hoarse and almost sad. "How long will you be in the area?"

"I really don't know. The future looks kind of fuzzy right now."

Jacob's eyes held a longing his lips lacked the courage to speak.

She touched his cheek then returned her hand to his. She had to know, but couldn't look him in the eyes. "Tell me about your wife."

Jacob released her and ran his fingers through his hair. He turned his face to the fire. "She left. What's more to tell?"

Ann touched his forearm. "I have feelings for you, Jacob. But before I risk my heart any further, I need to know you."

He tilted his head to the side and quirked a familiar smile. He was quiet for a thoughtful moment before he answered. "She claimed she had a nervous breakdown. From what, I honestly don't know. I thought everything was fine. She gradually withdrew though, until one day she packed up her things and left."

"Doesn't she have any contact with the children?"

"No." His jaw tightened. "She did at first. She was gone for three months and finally called, and then it was six months. I believe that call was an attempt to find out if I'd received the divorce papers. The last call was over a year ago. She called to tell me to sign the papers and return them."

"Oh."

"In the divorce, she willingly gave up custody of our kids."

Outside the wind whistled, as if to emphasize the emptiness left in their abandoned hearts.

Shocked, Ann was at a loss for words. What causes a woman to walk away from her own children?

"That's why we don't have a phone. It was too much, especially for Ethan. Every time it rang, he hoped it was his mom." Rubbing his chin he added, "I've ran it over and over in my head, and I don't know what I could've done different. I think something just snapped, you know, up here." He tapped his head.

"Do her parents still visit the children?"

"No. They ran after her. In their mind, she's still their baby who needs nurturing. I stopped trying to understand it. Her mom was always kind of silly, too."

Ann looked away. "I'm sorry for you and the children. It must've been hard to accept."

Jacob cupped her cheek in his hand and looked directly into her eyes. "I don't dwell on the past, I look to the future."

♡♡♡

How am I ever going to let her go?

The children lay asleep in a tangle of quilts while Ann slept curled up a few feet away. Her hand, still outstretched, held on to Jacob's. Something always held him back from admitting how he truly felt. His sudden vote of confidence in the field, when he told Ann he wouldn't back down, surprised him. But how far would he be willing to take their relationship? She wasn't at all like his first wife, but he played for keeps, and he couldn't face another rejection. How could he fully trust any commitment she might admit to?

A scripture from Hebrews jumped to mind. "Now faith is the substance of things hoped for, the evidence of things not seen." *Faith; that must be what I'm lacking.* Something deep inside ached to escape. Was it time for him to open up to God again? Not knowing why, Jacob continued to fight the urge to pray. Stubbornness had become such a part of him it was second nature to put up a wall to any help that might be offered. He nuzzled closer to Ann and slipped off into a fitful sleep.

Outside, the wind's howl died to a dull, eerie moan. Jacob and Ann bolted up. He was sure he heard something this time. From the look of fright on Ann's face, so had she. He froze and listened. It happened again. A horrid screech mixed with a deathlike moan. Chills climbed down his spine.

Ann paled. Her voice trembled. "Did you hear that? Someone's screaming!" She raced for the door.

Jacob reached her before she flung it open and grabbed her shoulders. He forced her to turn and look at him. "Stop and listen. I don't think it's someone at all but some, *thing.*"

Chapter Twelve

Although the darkness of night had faded into daylight, the screeching Ann heard remained in her thoughts. She twirled her hair as she sat at the table with Luke. "So you heard it, too?"

"Yep." Luke blew over his hot coffee. "I bet it was a female cougar. They'll scream like that when they're in heat. Only I didn't think we had any around. When Jacob contacted the conservation office about the calves, they said the only way we'd have a cougar in these parts is if it was passin' through. They were adamant there weren't any females to keep a male around."

"Maybe that agent should do some camping in your field."

Ann and Luke shared a laugh before his face turned more serious as he changed the subject. "I think Jacob's taken quite a liking to you."

Ann gave Luke her full attention. Her curiosity begged for more information. "Oh?"

Luke smiled. He must have known he'd hooked her. "Yep. There's been plenty of women folk try to snag his attention, but he's never been inclined to give it. In fact, I can think of a few at our church that's dropped hints and he just brushes them off." His eyes took on a twinkle. "But not you, Sunshine. And if my guess is right, he's the one that's dropped hints this time."

Ann couldn't suppress her smile. So, Jacob was a sought-after bachelor. What interested her most was the fact he hadn't pursued any of them. The, now, familiar flush crept up her neck. He had definitely pursued her. But for all his advances he never pushed her to the extreme, a fact she was grateful for. Because at the rate she was going, she may not make the right decision if it ever came to that.

God, I've not remembered to pray often enough. You've brought me through some rough water and for that I'm forever thankful. Please give me the wisdom to use the strength you've already supplied me with whenever my flesh is weak. Help me to live for you and edify you in all I do. Amen.

The peace that settled over her last night, still lingered. Talking with Jacob had relieved her of the burdens that'd weighed her down for the last two months. Who would've known the cynical farmer would be the perfect one to talk to?

The morning passed quickly and left Ann pleased with the children's eagerness to work with her. Since the creek was up, they weren't able to go to the Stevenson's for school. Instead, she schooled them. Though Emily showed more interest in learning than Ethan, he proved himself reliable enough to finish what she assigned him.

Ann stood from the table and straightened their books. "Okay, time for a break."

Ethan flew from his chair. "Whoo-hoo. I'm going outside."

"Not without me, you're not." Emily tripped around her seat and followed her brother.

She was Ethan's constant shadow, though it appeared he was never bothered by her presence. Ann admired him for that, but her heart also sympathized. Many times it appeared he felt the need to take on a more mature role. She credited it to the absence of their mother, and wondered how their lives would be affected if ever that role was filled.

A clock chimed and brought Ann out of her reflections. Knowing everyone would be hungry at lunch she'd started a roast early that morning. Its smell began to waft through the house and reminded her it was time to add the potatoes and start the vegetables.

"Wow. Jacob, you're one efficient farmer." Ann spoke out-loud to herself as she looked in the cupboard. "Who cans all these colorful vegetables?"

Had his mother been the one who canned, and who would teach that art to Emily now that she was gone?

The freezer was also well stocked. After she chose the frozen corn as an accompaniment to the canned green beans, she peeled potatoes. Ann looked through the window above the sink and watched the children run back and forth across the yard. She glanced back and saw Ethan with a shovel. Hmm . . . I bet that's why I tripped in a hole my first night here. The thought caused her to smile as she continued to prepare lunch.

♡♡♡

The water was a rush of torrents as it pushed itself along. Jacob stood near the edge, disheartened the bridge was still intact. It crested that morning, which meant it would be down enough by midday tomorrow he'd be able to take Ann home. With a heavy heart, he turned his attention back to the farm. He had cattle to check and the 180 acres wouldn't be easy to cover with all the rain they'd received.

Jacob drove out to the field and spotted a pregnant cow near the fence line. He could tell she wasn't able to birth the calf on her own. This was always one of the more challenging parts that went with this time of year, herding an expectant cow to the barn. He never had found one to be obliging.

"I hate pulling calves." Jacob sighed and turned the truck around. He returned to the barn to open the pen and ready the chute. He gave a hopeful glance in the direction of the house. If his dad saw him set up the chute with grain, he would know what it meant and possibly offer his aid.

The door never opened. Just as well really. Dad won't be around forever.

He returned to the field and honked the horn while he drove behind the pregnant cow. He hoped to start her in the direction of the barn. Needless to say, the cow didn't share his idea. She swung her cumbersome body to the right and plowed through the underbrush that claimed the edge of the field before the terrain dropped to a small ravine.

Jacob hopped out of the truck and grabbed a long stick. He proceeded to act like a man possessed as he ran about shouting and poking to get the stubborn cow back to the field. As he chased her through what he hoped wasn't tick-infested under growth, he was reminded of yet another chore to add to his list, brush hogging. When he thought he coaxed the cow in the right direction, she surprised him with a sharp turn and brushed past before she staggered down the steep embankment, sending a cascade of rocks clinking down the ravine.

Jacob bent over and rested his hands on his knees to catch his breath. As if his time with Ann wasn't short enough, this cow was determined to compromise it even more. He slowly walked to the edge and peered down to judge his next move. The cow stopped half way down the path. Her nostrils flared as she breathed in and out. Jacob shook his head and headed for the truck to grab a good length of rope. If she made it completely down the ravine it would likely be nightfall before the chase ever ended, thus endangering her and the unborn calf. Not wanting to risk the loss of yet another life, he'd have to rappel a distance ahead and flush her back up.

He secured his rope to the nearest tree and slowly rappelled down the steep incline. The cow raised her head. She blew angrily and pawed the ground. Jacob held his breath, could this have been a bad decision? Then, as if she were pulled by a lead rope, she backed up. As the path widened, she turned around. Jacob followed a few yards behind. When the cow was finally far enough past the truck, he reclaimed the driver's seat and drove after her. To any untrained eye, it would have looked as though he were intoxicated, with his constant swerving and speed. But it was a technique that proved itself time and again.

As he neared the open pen, Jacob gunned the truck, drove up beside her and blocked the only exit. He switched off the engine and ran after her. Although his feet were slowed as they met the muck and mire of the pen, he was still able to corner her into the head chute and shut the gate. Retrieving his tools from the truck, he started in on the next step.

His dad had recently bought a calf-puller, assured it would ease the job of pulling calves on his own. Time wasn't on Jacob's side and after losing a few minutes struggling with the tool, he threw it to the ground.

Frustrated at its awkwardness, he commenced to using a rope. He tied a bow knot on one end, then searched for the calf's front hooves and looped it around. He cinched it tight and pulled.

The calf was lodged in tight. Jacob strained and pulled with more strength. If too much time lapsed, the calf would suffocate and die. That is, if it hadn't already. The rope was already wrapped around his hand several times; he now added a loop over his shoulder and heaved backward. The calf's legs slid out. A few more tugs and the large newborn slumped to the ground. It struggled to stand; surprising Jacob it still had breath.

"Hello there, wobbly legs. I was beginning to doubt if you'd make it. Glad you did though."

Jacob swiped the sweat from his forehead with the sleeve of his arm. He'd always been too stubborn to know when to quit. Today, it paid off. And if his wife had given him the chance, it would've then, too. He pushed the memory aside. His marriage had failed. He had failed.

He opened the chute and watched the mother cow make her way over to nuzzle her new calf. Once assured it could suck properly, he released them into the field and washed off at the outside spigot. Satisfied with the results he headed back toward the house.

The former task having consumed his morning, Jacob looked forward to stopping for lunch. He wasn't driven so much by hunger as he was by the desire to see Ann. It surprised him how quickly he'd become accustomed to her presence.

♡♡♡

Ann ran from the giggling girl, trying not to get away too easily. She was thankful Ethan had given her a break. She may be able to outrun a four-year-old, but the eight-year-old offered more of a challenge. His legs, long like his father's, could cover more ground than she expected.

Ann looked up to keep track of Ethan and saw him run to greet his dad. There was no mistaking their relation. Ethan not only looked like his father, but also copied his every mannerism.

"Dad, wait until you smell what's cooking, Ann fixed us lunch and even Grandpa says it's better than his cooking!"

"Well, how does Grandpa know? Has he snuck in the kitchen?" Jacob ruffled his son's hair.

"I guess so." Ethan jumped with excitement. "Ann's planned a scavenger hunt!"

Ann held the old green coat closed with her hands as she ran from Emily. Ethan jumped ahead and helped capture her for Emily's turn to tickle.

Ann giggled and struggled to free herself. She looked up and her gaze connected with Jacob's. Was the look in his eyes a reflection of the yearning she had for him?

Ann went down as the children toppled her. She squirmed and laughed as their fingers jabbed her ribs until Jacob enabled her escape. He helped pull her to a stance before stepping back then shoved his hands inside his pockets.

Jacob cleared his throat. "Ethan told me you made lunch."

She nodded and struggled to calm her breathing. The children had given her a work-out. "I did. But if you don't mind, I told them we could have the scavenger hunt before we eat." She pointed to the children who already looked for clues.

"In that case, let me get you something warmer first." Jacob motioned for her to follow him inside.

Ann followed behind Jacob and glanced down at her muddy knees. Her clothes had finished drying before Jacob came home. Luke had found an old pink sweat suit of his wife's and lent it to her so she could do her laundry. Though she was grateful, they weren't exactly complimentary to her figure. From the look of things, she'd have to repeat the chore tomorrow. She hoped she could work around Jacob's presence. She didn't want him to see her as a walking bottle of Pepto.

Jacob led her to his room and rummaged through the closet. She paused in the doorway until he beckoned her to his side. "Here, this will not only keep you warm but will go great with your eyes." He wiggled his eyebrows.

She wound her way around the small space between the bed and the wall. "Oh and that's so important." She smiled, then accepted the sweater and admired the handiwork. "Who knitted this? It's beautiful."

"My mom. She always had to be doing something with her hands." As Jacob talked he stepped around Ann to help remove her jacket.

"Thank you. It'll beat trying to hold that old thing together for sure." She pulled the sweater over her head then turned to exit but bumped into the bed.

"Oof." She toppled halfway over the mattress.

Jacob hovered over her, his eyes glinted with mischief. He supported his weight with one hand beside her shoulder and slowly trailed a finger down her cheek and throat with the other. "Not that it doesn't keep crossing my mind, too, but under the circumstances," his mouth crooked a smile, "I don't think we should."

Chapter Thirteen

Jacob found his dad at the stove raising the lid to one of the pans. "Didn't Mom always say whoever got caught with their hand in the cookie jar would be the one to wash it?"

Luke dropped the lid back on the pot before he replied, "Then I guess it's a good thing you stopped me. That way I can avoid dish detail." He inhaled deeply. "Smells just like Mom's cooking, doesn't it, Son?"

"Yeah, it sure does. What have you been doing this afternoon besides sneaking bites of food?"

Luke chuckled. "Oh, a little of this and that."

"I sure could've used your help out there today. I had to chase ol' Bessie around the field all morning before pulling her calf."

Luke patted his son's shoulder. "Sorry, I didn't see you. I was probably asleep in the recliner. Next time, come in and holler for me."

"Hope you mean it. I'm sure there be plenty more opportunities."

Luke looked out the window. "You know it's a shame Tommy's not visiting. He'd be great to have around when you decide to hunt that wild cat."

Jacob didn't mind the change of conversation. It was something he'd given thought to as well. "No doubt about that. He has the sharpest eye of anyone I know."

Just wish he kept a better eye on his personal life. Jacob wasn't sure his dad knew how turned around Tommy's life had become. He'd always viewed the eldest of the Stevenson's children as the younger brother he never had. When Tommy made the decision to move away, Jacob vowed to visit. But with each trip, it became more evident what path Tommy had chosen. Between his weakness for women and his desire to party, the third visit became Jacob's last. Though he was aware his own walk with the Lord wasn't where it needed to be, he assumed Tommy no longer held to any belief.

Ann and the children stepped through the doorway with the energy of spring.

"Go wash up, then we'll eat," Ann told them.

As the children made their way down the hall, they kept a constant chatter directed toward Luke and Jacob. Jacob had washed and changed from helping the calf and now sat at the table.

Before Luke took a seat, he offered coffee to Ann. "You'll need this to keep up with those two." He smiled as he pointed in the children's direction.

Jacob couldn't take his eyes off Ann. Her cheeks had taken on a bright rosy hue from the crisp spring air and she radiated the same enthusiasm as the children. Her presence brought an unexpected completeness to his family. He'd never tried to fill the vacant spot the children's mother left. Though there were a few single women at church that expressed their interest, he didn't want to marry just to give the children a stepmother. But Ann, he realized, would never be seen as a stepmother. The children would eagerly accept her as their own, which is why he had to be careful and slow his feelings enough to fully consider the implication of his actions.

Lunch passed quickly as everyone eagerly devoured the wholesome meal Ann prepared. Jacob eyed the kitchen counters more than once but wanted to wait until after the meal to tease Ann about the mess. Just in case she didn't take it well, he didn't want to lose his plate of food.

"Now you know, Annie, we all loved the meal. But I just have to ask," Jacob perused the countertops again. "How in the world did you manage to make such a huge mess with just one dinner?"

He admitted the kitchen didn't offer much counter space, but what it did offer was now consumed with every imaginable dish and utensil. A trail of milky cornstarch rings traveled from the counter to the stove where gravy splattered the oven's surface. Empty jars and freezer bags dirtied the sink. Yet, as messy as it was, he wasn't upset. If anything, he felt honored Ann would go to such obvious means to impress them.

Ann laughed, a beautiful sound, and hung her head. "I know it's terrible. That's how I've always cooked. It drives my mother crazy. But you'll be pleased to know I clean up as good as I mess!"

Luke carried his plate to the counter. "Well, let me wash the dishes at least, and then I'll get out of the way so you can finish school. A little kitchen duty won't hurt for having just eaten the best meal I've had in a long time."

Jacob watched his father and Ann work together as he laced on his boots. His father had taken an immediate liking to Ann, which he didn't keep secret. Jacob understood the hints but tried not to encourage him. Though looking at them now, he couldn't help but smile.

"Dad, before you get lost in that mess, why don't you leave those girly chores alone and come out and help me?"

Ann spun on her heels and narrowed her eyes at Jacob. Her expression relaxed when she saw his smile.

"You sure your hair's not naturally red?" he laughed.

"All right, so you had me. But it's a lucky thing for you that you weren't serious."

Luke cut in, "Okay, we'll be outside if you need us, Sunshine." Before he left, he planted a light kiss on Ann's cheek and thanked her again for dinner.

♡♡♡

Jacob pulled himself out from under the tractor when Ann walked in. A warmth rose in his chest and he couldn't control the smile that greeted her.

"I brought you and Luke, coffee."

Jacob stood and brushed himself off. "That was thoughtful, but Dad went to check on Candy. We just finished up."

Ann's eyes narrowed. Was she aware of his dad playing matchmaker?

"Penny for your thoughts?" Jacob reached for a mug.

"It's nothing. But I do want to thank you. I hadn't intended to impose on anyone when I took off the other day in the truck. But I'm really glad everything happened as it did."

Jacob relaxed with his back against the tractor. He cocked his head sideways and furrowed his brows. "What is it? You have a funny look on your face."

Ann giggled. "You have a smidgen of grease on your nose."

Jacob took a swipe with the sleeve of his shirt.

"No, it's still there." Ann closed the space between them. "Let me."

She took the rag that hung from his belt loop and gently swiped at the grease. Jacob set his mug down beside hers on the tractor's step, and wrapped his hands around her narrow waist. "Taking care of me, are you?"

Ann looked up and bit her lip. What was she holding back?

"I went to the bridge today," Jacob secured his hands around her then added, "and I figure you'll be able to escape us tomorrow afternoon." Jacob waited to see her reaction.

Ann's head dropped and she turned to step away, only Jacob held fast to her. "Look at me, Annie."

"No, I . . . uh . . . I . . ."

Gently, Jacob cupped her chin and forced her to look up. His gut wrenched with the sadness revealed in her eyes. He knew the tenderness he felt for her was revealed in his own and did nothing to hide it. Without speaking, he tilted his head and brushed his lips to hers before pulling her close. He stroked her hair as he rested his chin on top of her head.

Jacob didn't have any answers. The miles between them weren't many, but how long would Ann be in the area. Her stay was only meant as a retreat.

Jacob pulled back and said, "Today is what, Monday? It's hard to keep track with missing church and all that's gone on," he nervously rubbed his chin. "Anyway, how would you like to spend Sunday with us? We could pick you up for church and have the rest of the day together. You aren't planning on leaving Missouri any time soon, right?"

"No, I'm here until my relatives get back from their trip. Sunday would be nice. I'd love to." Ann's smile was weak as she backed toward the door. "I'd better get back inside. Ethan may need help with his project."

"What project would that be?" Anything to keep her there talking with him.

Ann responded over her shoulder as she continued toward the barn door. "He wants to surprise you. You'll see when you come in."

Jacob now stood alone with two cups of cold coffee. Hadn't he set up another date? Why did she still seem distant? There should be a class guys could take on how to read women's minds. He released a long sigh and wiped down his tools. How in the world would he be able to wait six days until he saw her again? He couldn't. He had to think of an excuse to visit sooner.

♡♡♡

Ann slowly walked to the house. Though numbness had replaced all emotion, she still fought back the stinging of tears. She appreciated the offer to spend the day with Jacob's family on Sunday. But when she went home tomorrow, it would be six more days before she'd see him again. Six long days . . . yet, he was willing to wait 'til then. Didn't he feel the same way she did?

Obviously, not.

God, I know this is foolish to get so emotional over something probably not as important as I'm making it out to be. But it hurts so much to not be wanted the same way in return. I thought you desired for me to be single. I accepted that, even though it wasn't what I wanted. Then it seemed as though you were gifting me with a family, but if he can wait six days to see me again . . . what does that say?

She sucked in a deep breath of cold air and swiped at her eyes before opening the door. Ethan had finished

118

his project and was preoccupied somewhere else. Thankful for the extra time alone, Ann rummaged around in the kitchen for ideas for dinner. Though she sensed God tug at her heart, this time she refused to give in. She would love to fall down on her knees and cry her heart out to Him, but if she did, someone would surely walk in on her during her moment of weakness. Forced to admit her broken heart and empty dreams aloud would only complete her devastation.

Try as she might, the feelings that nagged her wouldn't let up. She wanted to clear her head, so she left the children with Luke and explained her need for a walk. Ann headed in the direction of the old barn she had seen on her drive over and reminisced about her childhood days when family reunions held as much excitement as an amusement park.

Every year her aunt and uncle cut a maze in the cornfield and stacked straw bales in the barn loft to create tunnels and secret passages that were always different from the year before. She could never count the endless hours she'd spent playing there.

Ann remembered a particular occasion in the loft when she and three cousins hid in their secret room and discussed what they would be when they grew up. Sadie was going to be nothing less than a cowgirl and compete in rodeos; that had been her most recent phase. Teresa had her hopes set on a nursing profession. Natalie, Ann's closest cousin, was bound for Hollywood. Ann had felt foolish with her desires in comparison to her cousins' big dreams. She'd silently held back her hopes of simply being a mother and steered them away from prying into her thoughts with a clever turn to humor, as a way of avoiding deceit. She claimed she would be the clown the bull chased in an effort to keep Sadie safe.

Ann surprised herself by laughing out loud. She imagined herself dressed as a clown, with polka dots and a big red nose, scared out of her mind as she madly ran from a furious bull. Bravery wasn't one of her gifts.

Gone were the days when she assumed all her hopes and dreams would one day come true. Restless of not having a family of her own and not wanting to settle for less than love, she'd turned to being a nanny.

Until now.

Why did God call me back here and why is He taking so long in letting me know?

"Wait on the Lord. Be of good courage and He shall strengthen thine heart; wait I say on the Lord."

Again, Ann was thankful her aunt had drilled into her the importance of memorizing scripture. God's word sprung to mind right when she needed it most. She could almost hear Aunt Ellie as she told the story of Jesus being tempted and how He'd answered the devil with the words, "It is written . . ." referring to God's word. Her aunt would then add in her singsong voice, "If His word is a good enough defense for my Savior, then it's good enough for me!"

Ann stopped to catch her breath after cresting a hill and crept close to the edge of the road. She leaned around a sturdy young tree to steady herself and peered down. Past a sheer drop, she could see a flooded creek that flowed about fifty feet below. The sound of its rushing waters reminding her of why she was still here. The face of the cliff was dotted with rocks and trees and across the creek it quickly became forest again before it climbed into another hill. She pushed against the tree to turn back but something caught her eye. A couple of the trees looked blotted with white where their bark had been removed. They stood out like snow on ash. Ann wondered if it had been caused by a large buck rubbing his antlers.

She straightened and rubbed the goose-bumps on her arms. It was a long way down. What if she'd fallen?

Up ahead, on the other side of the road, she could see the barn. At one time it had probably been surrounded by fields, but was now partially hidden by a young forest. She turned her wobbly knees in that direction, thankful to leave the cliff.

Ann paused in the road and reflected on the lost character the old barn represented. It stood as a testament of a time and lifestyle of a bygone era, when communities depended on one another to survive and expected to be called upon to help. Unlike now, where it seemed people no longer needed those they lived around to be successful, therefore neighbors were all but forgotten, just like this old barn.

Ann made her way through the trees and soon stood in front of the forgotten monument. Towering oak planks, gnarled and twisted with age, invoked a feeling of awe. She took a timid step inside.

Where pieces of tin had blown off the roof, a ray of sunlight had reached a fallen acorn, resulting in the half-grown tree that now grew from the inside out. Sliding back a wooden latch, Ann stepped into a hall that separated two larger compartments. Excited about the prospect of what she might find, she peered through the space between two boards.

Covered by a layer of dust, stood the remains of an old Model A. She might not have known what it was, if it weren't for the one owned by her grandfather. She located the door into the stall and stepped toward the car as though going back in time. Her finger trailed through decades of dust on the hood as she walked around and admired the old wire grill. Though it was still intact, the bumper had been dented and the front right headlight was missing. She continued to the other side and slid behind the car and wall. Her jeans snagged on the bumper and drew her attention to a plate last licensed in '76.

"Hmm, forgotten in time are you?" Ann absently spoke out loud, as she took in the nostalgic atmosphere created by the dim, broken light. Old tools hung on the adjacent barn wall along with ropes of twine and a broken bridle. The stories this old place could tell.

The light changed, as if a shadow passed by. Ann's breath froze. "Is someone else here?"

Above, loft boards creaked. Dust sprinkled into the shafts of light around her. Her mind raced as a rapid pounding claimed her heart. Don't panic. She forced a breath against the tightening of her chest.

Frantic eyes searched for an exit. The stall door held her only escape. Ann took shallow breaths as she moved toward the other side of the room, sawdust softened her footsteps. Once there, she paused and nervously twirled her hair.

The open front of the barn stood partially visible. Ann strained to see or hear something . . . anything outside the opening. She started forward.

Thump.

A startled shriek escaped her lips.

Had something heavy fallen from the loft?

She held her breath. A crash followed a blur of movement. Something large made a quick retreat.

Ann screamed.

Another thump sounded. Something heavy approached on the wooden floor. Ann screamed again and turned to run. She whirled and tripped over her own feet. She tried to crawl toward the safety of the old car but something snagged her jeans. Her pulse sounded in her ears as panic pushed tears from her eyes.

Jacob burst through the opening. "Annie, Annie!" He picked her up, unsnagging her jeans from barbed wire.

Ann collapsed in Jacob's arms and began to weep. "I'm so sorry. I forgot about the cougar, and—and I saw something and got sc-scared and didn't know what to do."

Jacob held her to his chest. "Come on. Let's get you home so I can give you the scolding you deserve."

Chapter Fourteen

Jacob led Ann to Trigger, tied by the road. When he moved to help her up, the horse shied away. "Well, what's got you so worked up?"

Jacob rubbed the horse's neck and turned him around a couple of times before he tried again, this time succeeding. Though he didn't want to give an already frightened Ann reason for more hysterics, Jacob could tell the horse was spooked. What had scared him? What if Ann had really been in danger? Frustration gnawed away. Ann's stubbornness could have gotten her hurt. If what had frightened her and the horse was the cougar, would it have attacked her to defend its den? Jacob didn't know, but one thing for sure, he couldn't stand the thought of her being hurt. He kept his thoughts to himself and avoided conversation until his home came into view.

Then he asked the question eating away at him. "What gave you the hair-brained idea to go off by yourself knowing the dangers around here?"

"I'm not in the mood for lectures. In fact, stop the horse, I want off."

"Not a chance. You must have gotten your senses spooked out of you back there. Now, what were you doing?"

"Taking a walk."

"Alone, without a rifle. Not the smartest thing to do."

"And, what's it to you? I'll be out of your hair tomorrow. Then you won't have to worry about me anymore, except for the church thing on Sunday. You can still cancel if you want."

"Not on your life."

Silence. Did she want him to bale? Did she think he was glad she was leaving?

When they reached the cabin, Ann swung her leg over the neck of the horse and dismounted before Jacob.

"Women," he muttered, as he unsaddled his mount and watched her stomp into the house.

Jacob entered through the back door a few minutes later, and spied Ann cutting out biscuits on the counter. Although she greeted him politely, she wouldn't bring her eyes to meet his. He'd stayed outside to tend the animals and give her time to get over being upset. It hadn't been enough.

"Hey, Dad. Look at my castle." Ethan proudly showed off his popsicle-stick craft.

Jacob leaned over the kitchen table and examined the drawbridge. "I'm impressed. Really impressed. You have talent, Son."

Emily emerged from her room and ran passed Jacob's open arms. She hugged Ann's waist and looked up.

"Do you want to help, Sweetie?" Ann didn't need to ask for a chair. Jacob anticipated her need and pulled one to the counter as Emily climbed up. He barely heard Ann's thank you before she showed Emily what to do. He was glad she could keep a sweet tone when talking to his kids, even though she'd lost it toward him. He sighed and walked back outside, glad to see Ethan follow him. At least he still had one fan.

Dinner passed without incident. Though any conversation Ann directed toward Jacob was stinted and void of feeling, at least she hadn't ignored him completely. He brought in firewood for the night while Ann stayed busy in the kitchen. Supposedly, with clean-up.

Jacob walked up beside her and took the broom. "Would you stop and rest? You haven't sat still all evening."

Catching her glance before her eyes fell to the floor, Jacob's heart fell with them. In that fleeting moment, he recognized the raw pain he often saw in his own reflection. He took her arms in his hands and turned her toward him. "What's bothering you, Annie?"

Her eyes fell back to the floor. "Nothing, I'm fine. But I am tired, so I think I'll call it an early night." She eased away from his grip and walked toward his children. His arms dropped to his sides. Somehow they were emptier now, than they were before he held her.

"Annie."

"Goodnight, kids. I'm heading to bed early, but I'll see you in the morning." They exchanged hugs before Ann turned down the hall and closed the door to her room.

The sudden stillness in the house felt unnatural. Ethan and Emily looked at him with questioning eyes. Though Ann had only been with them for a few nights, they were already accustomed to being together.

Emily asked, "What do you want to do, Dad?"

"Yeah, I'm bored." Ethan dropped a puzzle piece back to the floor.

"I think we'll all go to bed early."

Ethan rose without complaint. "Good, 'cause it's no fun without Ann."

The children walked down the hall to ready themselves for bed. Jacob ran a hand through his hair. Bored? How could they be bored? Their evenings had always been just the three of them. But what had they done? His mind was so focused on Ann he couldn't remember.

♡♡♡

The clock struck one and Jacob realized he'd never be able to sleep unless he talked to Ann. He walked down the hall and rested his temple on her door. Softly, he rapped his knuckle against it. "Annie, I know you're awake, too. We need to talk."

He didn't hear a response and knocked again. How could she sleep? He cracked open the door intent on waking her.

Ann gasped, "What are you doing?"

"Why didn't you answer?" His voice was irritated.

"I was going to put my jeans on and come out." She wore his button-down shirt and held the jeans in front of her.

Jacob sighed and walked in. He opened his mouth to say something when Ann cut him off, "Do you mind?" She asked, as she held her jeans higher.

"Give me those." Jacob jerked them from her hands and tossed them on the bed. "You didn't have them on the other night, why be shy now?"

Ann tilted her chin upward. "I would have if I'd known you were on the couch." She grabbed her jeans, brushed past him, and walked out of the room.

Jacob softened his voice as he followed her. "Look Annie, I didn't come in there with the intent to ruffle your feathers."

She closed the bathroom door in his face.

A few moments passed and it reopened with Ann in her jeans. Her eyes widened to see Jacob had waited for her in the hall. She sighed and headed toward the living room.

Jacob followed close behind. "You would hardly meet my eyes all evening and I can't seem to be able to think, eat, or sleep knowing you're upset with me." He exhaled and ran his fingers through his hair.

Ann shifted her feet and looked at the floor as if it would offer her wisdom.

Jacob reached for her and pulled her closer. He rubbed her cheek with the back of his hand. "I'm not leaving you alone until you tell me what's bothering you." He traced the length of her arm and pulled her closer, still.

She leaned into him before she gave her head a slight shake, and pulled back. He kept his hold and searched her eyes.

She was afraid.

"Annie, I'll never do anything to hurt you. Tell me what it is."

She rested her head on his chest and sighed. "Jacob," she paused and drew in a deep breath. "I can't stand the thought of being away from you and your family for one day—" her voice cracked, "and you're willing to put me off for six." She gave in to the small sobs that waited to escape.

"Oh, Annie." Jacob smiled as he took her up in his arms and sat down on the side of the couch. Gently, he pried Ann's hands away from her face. "Please don't hide. I love it that you would miss us that much. Though, I selfishly hope it's more me than anyone else."

He waited for her response then took her silence as consent. "The truth is, I spent extra time in the barn trying to figure out an excuse to see you sooner. I'm sorry I couldn't come up with anything better the first time. I'm on unfamiliar ground here."

Ann released a small hiccup. "I'm sorry I didn't handle myself better. I thought I could reign in my emotions before you caught on, but I should've known better." As she wiped her eyes, she added, "My mother always told me not to wear my heart on my sleeve, but I guess I never knew where-else to hide it."

He lifted her chin so he could clearly see her eyes. "That's good to hear, that way I'll always know if something's wrong, and I can fix it before it becomes a problem."

"Always?"

"Always." Jacob kissed her solidly.

Having her close once more was all the excuse he needed to give in to the desires that tempted him since her arrival. He deepened his kiss, yet, still yearned for more. His fingers laced through her hair and pulled her head back far enough to expose her tender neck. He trailed kisses along her shoulder to her ear and nibbled her lobe. Ann sighed and reached around Jacob to draw him closer.

Not wanting to acknowledge where they were headed, they continued with more intensity. Jacob eased back against the cushions and brought Ann with him.

What was he doing?

Convicted, he paused. The last thing he wanted was to disrespect Ann. And why should he behave this way now, when he never had in the past? His first wife had been the only woman he ever dated and they'd respected the Bible's instructions about fleeing from sexual immorality. But there was something about Ann that caused his brain to go dead, and his body to shift into overdrive.

She deserved better. He released his possessive hold.

Ann whispered, "Thank you."

"I like you, Annie, a lot. And not only do I never want to hurt you, I also don't want to disrespect you." He paused. "Would you mind if I just held you in my arms for a while?"

She nestled next to him as his hand lovingly caressed her hair.

♡♡♡

Jacob had held Ann next to him until she'd fallen asleep then carried her back to her room and took his designated spot on the couch. Raw emotion surged through him. His desires had suddenly changed from selfish and lustful to something he couldn't quite describe.

Dawn broke as he tried to put her from his thoughts long enough to concentrate on chores. He planned to drive Ann home but still needed to retrieve one of the wheels from her uncle's truck to have the tire repaired. That, along with his normal routine, would easily occupy him well up to noon.

Jacob still didn't want her to leave. But what he could say that would give Ann the assurance she needed? Marriage? What woman wouldn't run at the notion after only three days of knowing each other?

And, did he even love her? His head began to pound. This was entirely too much pre-coffee thought. He shoved his feet into his weathered boots and hurried outside, in hopes the new day would shine some light into his troubled soul.

Jacob peered across the field at the changing landscape. Winter was slowly giving way to spring, proving itself by forming tiny buds at the end of desolate branches that lined the rolling pasture and any spot that hadn't been cleared. He should see this as a sign of rebirth and hope. Instead, it reminded him of his past.

It had been a day much like this when his wife walked out. He'd never understood what drove her to walk away from him, but accepted it. What he couldn't accept, was how she was able to walk away from their children . . . and never look back.

Though the memory was painful, it was one he often relived. Ethan, their six-year-old son, had stood by his side without a sound and watched his mother throw her belongings into an old suitcase. Two-year-old Emily picked up on the tension and followed their mother around the house, crying and begging to be held. Every time Jacob tried to comfort her, she would squeal and cry, "Mommy, Mommy!"

When the car finally started out the driveway, Ethan broke away from his father's side and ran after her yelling in drawn out words, "Don't—leave—us!" He ran until his mother's car was out of sight then dropped to his knees. He'd drawn in ragged breaths of air in between each cry. The sound of his broken heart still weighed heavily on Jacob's.

Somehow, he'd failed.

Jacob and his children had made it for two years and thanks to the help and support of his father, they would continue to survive. But this morning, he sensed it was his Heavenly Father that wanted to help. Slowly, a verse from his youth sprang to mind, "Lean not on thy own understanding, but in all thy ways acknowledge Him and He will direct your path."

That was exactly what Jacob had not done. When Elizabeth walked out of his life, he'd shut God out, too. Though he still went to church every Sunday out of routine: the children would go to Sunday school: he would sit in the pew through service. He kept his heart cold and refused the comfort of the Lord. Why? Did his sense of failure lead him to think God would no longer love him? Or was it a way to punish himself, considering he must have been a lousy husband or Elizabeth would have stayed? Knowing the latter was closer to the truth, Jacob allowed the familiar doubt to rise again as he thought of Ann.

Would he fail her, too?

Chapter Fifteen

The morning proved cool and damp, the air hung like a thick web. Sleep prickled his legs like needles, but Elijah Stevenson fought the urge to move. He'd ventured out early to scout for turkeys before opening season. If he was correct, he'd beaten the fowl before they left their roosts, thus giving him the edge. The dawn just made its crest, now all he had to do was stay alert.

A mysterious aura surrounded him. Goosebumps prickled his skin for no reason at all. He often prided himself for being mature for his 14 years, yet found his bravado in a decline on this particular morning. Movement from his left caught his attention. He froze. Was it a turkey? Would his efforts pay off? He released the breath he'd unconsciously held, and waited as still as possible. As time ticked away, silence was the only response, as if everything had suddenly frozen over. Had it been this quiet before? Unwilling to allow his fears to become false illusions, Elijah forced himself to relax. Although, he still had a vulnerable feeling of being watched.

After what seemed an eternity, his patience finally won out. Over the ridge, he heard the familiar call of a gobbler as he descended from his roost. Elijah made a mental note of its position and listened for the expected answering calls.

Snap!

Off to his side and behind, a small branch broke from beneath the weight of its trespasser. Now Elijah knew he wasn't alone. Since he was doing preseason scouting, he'd left his shotgun at home. His unease grew. He shifted his weight to ease his escape should he need to leave quickly. Moments passed while he debated his next course of action when a group of birds moved upon him from his right. They were led by an impressionable-sized gobbler, unaware of Elijah's presence. Entranced by their magnificence, his attention became absorbed in their display.

A hen turned her head to peer past Elijah and made a "put" sound to alarm the flock of possible danger. Several of the other birds surveyed the dense foliage with beady, anxious eyes. What started as one "put", turned into several as the birds sensed a danger unforeseen by the boy. He stiffened, unsure what to do. A noise sounded. Then a large blur shot from the undergrowth and scattered the flock to the air and trees.

Dominated by fear, Elijah leaped from the ground and sprinted as fast as his legs would allow. He didn't dare look back as he pushed his body to its limits. His lungs burned as if they would burst from the strain. He broke forth from the trees but didn't stop until he flung the backdoor open and collided with his mother.

"What in the name of all that's good has gotten into you?"

Breathless, Elijah fought to reclaim his composure. "I—I have chores to finish before school, that's all."

♡♡♡

Ann awoke with mixed feelings. It was clear Jacob was attracted to her, but she wanted the whole deal. And though she had opened up to him, he'd never given the full assurance she needed.

Her limbs seemed weighted as she went about the morning. The children were too distracted to concentrate well on school. Again, Emily crawled onto her lap and leaned against her. "I wish you would stay forever, Miss Ann."

What could she say? Sunday had already been mentioned but it had provided as little comfort to the children as it had Ann. It still stood six days away.

Ann lifted Emily from her lap and set her on the couch. "Let's read together."

Ethan shuffled in and stood a few feet away. "I remember my mom reading to me. But that was before Sis was born, before mom changed." A deep sadness blanketed his gaze. "She never came back . . . are you coming back?"

Ann blinked rapidly and forced her voice to cooperate. "Of course I'm coming back." She would, too. No matter what happened between her and Jacob, she wouldn't break these children's hearts.

She managed to get through the morning without shedding any tears. But as noon approached, her heart weighed her down. Jacob had left as usual, before anyone was up. That meant she hadn't had a chance to talk to him. Without his reassurance, doubts attacked her mind. What is he thinking? Does he feel the same or is he having doubts?

When Jacob returned and washed up, the children and Luke were at the table ready to eat. They all knew he would drive her home after lunch. Perhaps that was the reason for the unusual silence. Ann couldn't even make small talk. Every time she looked at the family that wasn't hers, emptiness sprang in her heart.

As she said her goodbyes to the children and Luke, Ann fought back tears that struggled for release. Emily made no such effort as she ran back into the house.

Ethan was a replica of his father and kept himself unreadable. He snuck a drawing into Ann's hand before he gave her a quick embrace. Luke kissed her lightly on the cheek and with more confidence than the rest of them combined, said, "We'll be seeing you soon, Sunshine. Of that, I'm sure!"

♡♡♡

At seven years of age, Joseph Stevenson often grew restless seated in front of books. He relished every chance of being outdoors. When he was finally permitted to take a break from his studies, he bolted outside. Oblivious to the screen door as it slammed against the side of the house, he leaped off the porch in a dead run for his ball and bat.

Elijah stepped outside after him to finish his chores. "Don't get far from the house, Joseph."

"I won't." He threw his baseball in the air and swung. With his third pitch he connected and jogged to the edge of the yard to retrieve the ball. Movement beyond the trees caught his attention.

Joseph looked back to the house and saw his brother busy at the trash barrel. He spoke in a whisper to himself, "If you're a big buck, won't my brothers be surprised when I tell them I saw you. I won't even mind the switching from mother if you'll have more points than the one they saw."

Elijah walked to the house and called after his brother. "Joseph, get your ball and come on back."

"Ahh," he muttered as he kicked the ground and turned to obey. "I'm coming."

Gaunt with hunger, the young lion's lack of experience had proven to be his enemy.

The birds had ascended out of reach before he could claim one, which left him wasted of energy and desperate for a meal.

Elijah watched Joseph start toward the house. Without warning, the ravenous cat sprang from the thicket and upon his prey before the boy could cry out. The cat's teeth sunk into Joseph's lower skull and neck.

Horror stiffened Elijah's frame as the cat dragged his brother into the woods. "Nooo! Somebody get help– Joseph!" He raced toward the gruesome scene, stretching his legs their full width, slowing only long enough to grab the bat from where it lay on the lawn. The visual nightmare of his brother's limp body drug fearfully out of reach, squeezed his chest. Faster he raced, his trepidation turning into sheer speed.

Elijah swung at the savage cat and brought the bat down across his back. The lion's eyes retaliated with a menacing hatred as he lurched from the blow, yet continued his hold on the weakening boy.

Desperation threatened to drown Elijah as he swung again and again, demanding his brother's release. The cougar responded with a menacing growl and eerie yowling but never released the boy. Undeterred, the beast still fought to drag his prey toward thicker underbrush.

137

Elijah's arms ached from each swing of the bat and his lungs grew dry and sore. A haunting hopelessness consumed him. Tears streamed his face as he staggered backward and looked down at his brother. A cold shiver racked his body before he doubled over and vomited.

As the cat stared at Elijah in a silent stand-off, Joseph's eyes slowly opened. Elijah glanced over. His breath hitched as their eyes met. Joseph's pleaded for his rescue. Elijah watched as his brother painfully mouthed the words, help me. His eyes slowly drifted closed.

Elijah threw the bat over his shoulder and cried out, "Dear God in Heaven; help me!"

As though guided by an unseen force, his next strike connected with the blunt of the feline's nose. The cat reared back with a wail, released his victim, and retreated into the safe cover of the trees. Elijah collapsed to the ground in front of his little brother.

"Almighty God in Heaven," he heaved, "please place your healing hand on my brother . . ."

His mother's wail alerted him to her presence. She collapsed to the ground beside him, incoherent mutterings escaped her lips. Elijah had never felt so helpless. He stood and staggered backward as an older brother moved around him and scooped Joseph into his arms. The boy's limp body appeared so much smaller than Elijah remembered. He helped his mother struggle to her feet before they hurried to the house.

Once inside, her voice took on a sudden strength that surprised him. "Get lots of blankets. We have to prevent him from going into shock."

Elijah was relieved to see her regain control and take charge. Together they wrapped him in quilts before they fled to the hospital, an hour away.

♡♡♡

Ann sat beside Jacob in the truck and quietly opened the picture from Ethan. In front of a log cabin were three adults and two children, all of them held hands, with what appeared to be Jacob and Ann in the middle. Below was a picture of a dog and the words, "I hope we can be a real family one day." Her hands trembled as she refolded it and held it in her lap. She focused on the road and allowed the stinging in her eyes to pass.

The shadowy distance had fallen over them again. Ann knew they should talk but didn't want to push. Jacob covered her hands with one of his. "I don't want to wait until Sunday, Ann. I know I'd go crazy if I had to wait that long. Just give me a day or two to sort things out."

Ann swallowed and kept her attention on the road. "I'm not Elizabeth, Jacob."

With the mention of his ex-wife's name, Jacob's foot slipped off the gas pedal. He fumbled with his feet but failed to engage the clutch as he pressed on the brake. The truck engine died.

Ann's body lurched forward followed by a thump.

"Sorry. Did you hit your head?" Jacob cupped her face in his hand. Concern filled his eyes.

She rubbed her forehead. "Yeah, but I'm fine."

"How—where did you hear her name?"

She touched his arm as she said, "Ethan told me. But please don't think I was prying. He came up to me and started to talk on his own. I think he's sorting things out in his mind. Finding a way to make peace with the past and still move on."

139

Jacob nodded as he leaned against the steering wheel. "Sounds like I could learn a lesson or two from my son."

A car barreled onto the road in front of them and disappeared in a cloud of dust.

"Who was that?" asked Ann.

Jacob restarted the truck. "It looked like the Stevenson's car. We'd better make a detour and check on them."

Jacob turned at the next county road and drove past the few houses that shared the dead-end road with the Stevenson's. Jacob and Ann made their way to the door and were met by a harried boy with an overly distraught toddler in his arms. The boy ushered them in and nearly threw the girl into Ann's arms.

Ann turned to step back outside. The outdoors often calmed a child faster. The boy flung himself in front of her and barricaded the door with his body.

"You can't go out there." His wild eyed fear did nothing to help soothe his sister.

"Theodore." Jacob calmly took him by the shoulder and led him to the kitchen. "Sit down." He filled a glass of water. "Drink this and tell me what happened."

Ann overheard bits and pieces from the hallway. ". . . the cougar ran off . . . went to the hospital . . ." A shiver of fear ran up her spine. Whatever happened, no wonder the child in her arms was so distraught.

Upstairs, Ann softly hummed to a now sleeping Ruthie when Jacob found her. He motioned to her from the hallway. Ann laid the young girl in her bed and crept out of the room.

She rubbed her hands up and down her arms to smooth away her goose-bumps. "She was hysterical, what on earth happened?"

"A cougar attacked one of the Stevenson's sons."

Ann gasped and clasped her hands over her mouth.

"I know it's terrible. Be glad you weren't down there for the details. I have the boys in the living room occupied with books. As for the one in the hospital, all you can do is hope for the best."

"I can pray." Ann noticed Jacob tense ever so slightly. "You can, too, you know."

"You're probably better than me in that department."

Ann jerked her head back in surprise. "But I thought because of your comment about convictions and asking me to church that you . . ." Her voice trailed as an insurmountable disappointment filled her spirit.

"Ann, I have to go."

She was almost too afraid to ask, but did anyway. "Where are you going?"

"Huntin'."

Chapter Sixteen

Ann stood alone in the Stevenson's upstairs hallway. *What is wrong with that man?* She couldn't be with someone who didn't share her faith. But she'd been certain he did. *Would God bring them this far for nothing?* She ran down the stairs after him. "Jacob."

He turned as he was about to step through the Stevenson's front door.

"Jacob. I have to know what you meant. You can't just walk out of here like that."

A smile tugged at the corner of his mouth as he trailed the side of his finger down Ann's cheek. "I've given my heart to the Lord, Ann. I just haven't talked to Him much since Elizabeth left."

Ann kissed the inside of Jacob's palm before he pulled it back. "Then work on it. Okay?"

Jacob nodded. "You got it."

"And, hey, am I supposed to stay here while you hunt? 'Cause I don't recall being asked."

Jacob's smile broadened. "Yes, Sassy. Do you mind?"

"Not at all."

"Good, then I'll drop my kids off here, too, and Dad can hunt with me. I could use another set of eyes. Also, see if you can find the number to the conservation office and give them a call. Ask for, Jim. This should make a believer out of him."

Ann saluted. "Yes, Sir."

Jacob shook his head. "Thank you," he said, then made to leave.

"Jacob."

He stopped again and faced her. Ann flung her arms around his neck and kissed him. "Please be careful," she whispered in his ear.

♡♡♡

Nerves got the best of her. Ann had to do something. She opened the refrigerator and retrieved items for a stew. She had become her mother. At the first sign of stress, her mother always ended up in the kitchen. If someone was upset, she always tried to feed them. Oh well, it's not as though it's a bad trait.

Ann wiped the dinner table down when the phone rang. Her heart skipped a beat. Joseph. Would it be good news or bad? How would she be able to tell the children? God give me strength. "Hello?"

There was a pause on the other end before Mr. Stevenson's voice demanded, "Who is this?"

"It's Ann McHaven. I'm watching your children and Jacob's while he and Luke are hunting the cougar." She looked down at the mess she'd made of the phone cord and untwisted it from her fingers. Surely Mr. Stevenson wouldn't ask her to leave. She was, after-all, doing him the favor.

"Oh. Well I called to report the doctor's findings. I guess I can talk to you and you can tell my children. How are they, anyway?"

143

Ann drew a deep breath. "They're doing fine. Jacob's kids help to distract them. How is Joseph?"

"He's going to pull through." Ann could hear the pain in his voice as he continued. "He does have a slight fracture somewhere on the back of his neck. The doctor said he shouldn't be as stable as he is. The Good Lord was looking after him."

"Well, we've all been praying." Ann didn't know how to continue. She had so many more questions but they would have to wait. Perhaps next time she would be able to talk to his wife. Not only was she less formidable, but she would probably lend more information about Joseph's condition.

Mr. Stevenson drew the call to its end. "We'll call back when we know something else. How long do you plan to stay with the children, Ms. McHaven?"

"As long as I'm needed."

"Hmm, very well. Good night."

"Good night." The phone gave a dial tone and Ann looked at it curiously. She tried to hang it up, but the cord was wrapped several times around her wrist and fingers. She must have done that while talking to him and hadn't even noticed. "Ugg. Why do I feel like I'm standing in front of a principle to receive punishment whenever I talk to that guy?"

♡♡♡

The hunters' first attempt ran from mid-afternoon until dusk with little result. They resumed the hunt at first light and were now frustrated and tired from covering countless miles over rough Ozark terrain. Jacob and Luke, along with Jim the conservationist, began their return home.

"I'm looking forward to some coffee," Jim said as he released a huge yawn.

Jacob grumbled, "And some food."

Luke began to yawn in response, but stumbled on a root. Jacob was quick to catch him.

Luke smiled as he patted his son's back. "Nothing wrong with your reflexes."

"I think we all could use a—" He froze.

Jim and Luke followed his gaze to the remains of what looked like a cougar. The air was filled with the stench of stale blood and spray, possibly from a territorial cat.

Jim stepped forward and motioned to the others to keep an eye out. He approached the carcass and scanned the ground for silent clues. Willingly releasing its secrets, the forest floor was carpeted with signs of battle.

"I think this young fellow met his match with a much larger male. Judging from these tracks, I'd guess the winner weighs in around 170 pounds or more.

Jacob whistled from a little ways off and signaled he'd caught up with the trail of the other cat. "Look at the claw marks on this tree. They go right past my head."

"If I had to guess, this happened about three to four hours ago," Jim stood from beside the carcass. "Which makes sense, if you both will remember those eerie sounds we heard." Jim paused and released a shudder before he continued, "Makes me kind of glad we were so far off."

An ominous stillness fell amongst them. Not even a bird chirped. Finally, Jacob broke through the lull. "We're not getting any younger, so let's get this beast out of here."

After they dragged the cat back to the Stevenson's, Jim left with the carcass. He assured everyone he'd be in touch as soon as they had results from the rabies tests. Now a believer, he even told Jacob he'd form a hunting party for the larger cat that killed his stock.

Ann leaned against the door frame in the kitchen when Jacob entered. Luke had already cleaned up and snored fast asleep in an armchair.

"You look tired," he said as he caressed her arm.

Ann shrugged and walked to the counter to fill Jacob's plate. "I couldn't sleep last night, knowing you and your dad would be out there," her voice came out as a whisper, "with that, that monster."

Jacob encircled her from behind and pulled her into a protective embrace. He leaned closer to her ear and whispered, "'Fear not, for thou art with me, thy rod and thy staff they comfort me.' Isn't there a verse in Psalms that says something like that?"

Ann turned her head. "You surprise me."

"Oh, and why is that?"

She tucked the back of her head in the crevice of his neck and smiled. "Perhaps it's because when I first arrived, you threatened to take possession of me, and now you're quoting Bible verses. Kind of interesting is all."

"Hmmm, I see your point." Jacob drew her closer yet, and gently pushed her hair aside. He planted kisses on the inside of her neck. "Sadly, I have no excuse, and I find I'm still consumed with the thought."

Ruthie and Emily entered the kitchen and announced their need for food. Jacob sighed and heard Ann laugh at him.

"God's subtle reminders," she whispered.

Jacob shifted his feet as he cleared his throat. "I'll go wash up, then I'll get some breakfast."

How did she do it? Every time he came within five feet, he lost all control of his senses. At least he had a day of tracking planned. If he had to be around Ann for the whole day, he wasn't sure he could fight off temptation. Then again, the children offered constant interruptions. When he made her his wife, he'd plan a week away and have her all to himself.

Where did that thought come from, his wife? Is that what he wanted? If he was honest with himself, he never doubted her devotion; he was just giving an excuse to his fear. As if the idea suddenly landed on him at once, without a doubt, life without Ann would be far more terrifying than failing her. But when could he tell her? Every moment was interrupted by something or someone.

"Lord," Jacob silently prayed, "You know as much as I do how much I love Annie. Please show me the right time to tell her how I feel. And please give me strength, Lord. My flesh is weak. So very weak." When had he begun to pray again?

Ann sat down to eat with Jacob and the girls when the phone rang. She picked up the receiver. "Hello, this is the Stevenson's residence."

A short pause followed before Mr. Stevenson answered. "You're still there, huh? I thought you would have left by now."

She took a deep breath to contain her growing disdain and coolly replied, "I said I'd stay as long as I was needed."

After another pause, Mr. Stevenson said, "Hmm. It may seem I've been a bit hasty in forming an opinion of you, Ms. McHaven. When I called back to speak with Theodore last night, he mentioned all you've done. In fact, he read me a list. And for that, I'm thankful." He cleared his throat. "Please, forgive me."

Ann's jaw dropped, and Jacob gave her a curious look. "Of course, Mr. Stevenson." She then turned the conversation away from herself. "How is Joseph doing?"

"He's recuperating quite rapidly, but of course hasn't been released yet. Nevertheless, Mrs. Stevenson or I will return home today and our eldest son is coming home to lend a hand."

After a few more brief exchanges, Ann hung up the phone. "Joseph is doing really well and one of his parents will be home today."

Jacob rubbed a hand over his chin. "I can't believe he's pulled through so easily. The boy could have been paralyzed."

"See what prayer can do?"

Jacob studied her. "How about I take your smug and sassy self to your uncle's for a different set of clothes and then you stay with my kids until the hunt is over?"

Ann smiled at the opportunity to spend more time with them. "Sounds great. Oh, and I forgot to tell you, Mr. Stevenson's oldest son is coming home, too. That will give them an extra hand."

Jacob was glad Tommy Stevenson saw the importance of supporting his family in a time like this. Could they pick up where they left off? Perhaps Tommy would want to join in the hunt. The Lord knew Jacob could use his help.

His coffee cup paused at his lips.

Another thought occurred to Jacob, one not quite as peaceful. Tommy was a womanizer, with no respect of persons. Did he possess enough restraint to leave Ann alone? Most likely, not. More importantly, would Ann be swayed by Tommy's charms? Not able to control the sudden onslaught of frustration, Jacob made an excuse to step outside.

"Something bothering you, Son?"

"Dad. I didn't realize you were there."

"The ringing phone woke me from my sweet slumber." Luke smiled as he joined his son. "People are always changing, aren't they? Some for the worst, some for the best. And the hard part is keeping up with them."

Just how much did his dad know of Tommy's life style? Jacob waited for the wisdom his father was sure to impart.

"You want to know one of the things I've always appreciated about the disciples? They weren't perfect. They came from all sorts of backgrounds, and just because they walked with Jesus, it didn't make them perfect. They still made mistakes, even big ones like Peter's. But the Lord forgave them and by doing so, set a good example for us to follow."

"Something tells me you're not talking about the cougar."

His dad grinned. "I know you don't visit Tommy any more. I didn't figure it was any of my business to ask, but I noticed all the same."

"The kids probably said a little, too."

"That they did."

"Tommy's a hard one to figure, and I needed to hear what you said. Thanks, Dad." Jacob clapped his dad on the shoulder as they returned to the house. Feeling his heart lighten, he tried to stay optimistic.

♡♡♡

Jacob stretched his arms over his head then ran a hand over his stubbled jaw. A shower and a clean shave would feel good right about now. Into the second day of hunting the cougar and they weren't any closer to catching it than when they started. He glanced at his dad and saw the evident signs of fatigue around his eyes and in his stride. Though thankful for his help, the rough Ozark terrain was too much for him. Jacob needed to call it quits before his dad got hurt.

Once his dad was home, the excuse to have Ann stay would be nullified. Jacob had become accustomed to her presence. And, so had the children. Of course, if he hunted this evening, he would have the excuse for her to stay one more day. One less day of the house feeling empty.

Jim sighed loudly before his voice grated against the silence. "We need a team of dogs to corner this smart-alecky cat. This whole time we've been tracking it, I think it's been walking circles around us. I don't know about you two, but I'm tired of playing cat and mouse."

"I agree." Jacob's voice was rough from lack of sleep. "Let's head back to the cabin. Dad, why don't you check in with Candy and the family, and I'll get Moses."

Jim stared at him for a moment. "You mean your mutt?" His condescending tone said it all. They were physically and mentally drained.

Jacob squared his shoulders. "I don't recall the state of Missouri having a dog team set aside for tracking cats. So, just what do you suggest?"

"Well, I'm through for now. I'm beat and quite honestly, I'm tired of your company. I'll have a team ready to hunt this weekend."

Jacob shook his head and continued toward home. Aside from Jim's show of knowledge when they found the dead cougar, Jacob wasn't impressed with the man's credentials. If he was so smart, why hadn't they found a trace of the cat since the kill? The hunt was down to him. His dad needed a break, and Jim had made it clear he was tired of playing chase.

♡♡♡

Ann left the front door of Jacob's cabin open to allow the light to shine through the storm door as she gathered up the children's school books. It had been another productive day and the children were now outside playing. She hummed pleasantly to herself as she enjoyed the simple pleasure of keeping house.

She paused. The lighting in the room darkened. Ann caught the faint smell of expensive cologne before she turned to see a shadow loom in the doorway. "Aahhh!" The books fell from her arms with a loud thud.

"Excuse me, ma'am. I had no intention of alarming you." The young man had a natural charm about him and knew it. He eased the door open. "I'm Tommy Stevenson, the eldest son of Jacob's neighbors."

He stepped inside and extended his hand. The children ran to the door and shouted greetings to him. Their familiarity eased the tension from Ann's shoulders.

"Hi Tommy, I'm Ann. It's nice to meet you." He flowed with confident charm. Though it was easy to be drawn in, Ann had met his type before. She gave a polite smile but refused to give him anything more. She took a step back and studied him. He was tall and lean, and though his facial features weren't perfect, his smile drew them all together and made him attractive.

Though, if he expected his charms to work on her, he'd find himself disappointed.

Tommy brought his hand to his face and rubbed his cheek. "You probably wonder why I don't sport a beard like my father. He'd say it's because I'm rebelling against God." His eyes sparkled in a mischievous way. "I don't adhere to all their rules, so to speak."

A gruff voice came from behind Tommy. "I should've known to watch out for you."

The suave charmer spun around and looked sheepishly at Jacob who glared at him with obvious suspicion. Tommy extended his hand. "Hi, neighbor. I just had to come and see for myself. But no harm's been done."

"See what?" Ann asked.

He turned his attention toward her once more. "Why, you, of course. My siblings had plenty to say about their pretty baby-sitter. And since I didn't get an answer from the Garret's home, I assumed you were here. It seems you have a heart of gold to look after everyone's kids like you have. And naturally, I wondered if you didn't need a break. Perhaps a dinner that those overworked hands don't have to cook?"

He cast a look at Jacob as he leaned his shoulder against the door's trim. "I can't imagine Mr. Neanderthal knows how to properly treat a lady."

Without hesitation, Jacob grabbed Tommy by the back of his neck and thrust him out the door. Ann's jaw dropped before her hand covered her mouth.

"If what you came home for was to help your family, then I suggest you get back to it."

Chapter Seventeen

Jacob followed Tommy outside to keep him from saying too much. "Okay. You had your fun. Now, go home and help out like you're supposed to."

Tommy laughed so hard he nearly doubled over. "Man, can we say, pos-ses-sive? Jake, you've got it bad. And, it's about time."

"Mind your business, will you?" Jacob slapped Tommy on the back while projecting him toward his car. "So how's the little brother doing?"

"He'll survive. Do you think you're any closer to bagging the cat?"

"I'm fixin' to eat a bite and head back out. You want to come?"

Tommy's eyes lit with the same twinkle Jacob remembered from childhood. "You bet. But since I've driven and flown all day, you'll probably want me to get some shut eye."

"That's right. I don't want you to mistake me for the beast."

"Then it's settled. I'll see you at first light."

"That's if I don't get him tonight." Jacob watched Tommy stride the remaining distance to his car. It was a new high-end model with all the bells and whistles. No surprise. Tommy hadn't changed. The fact he drove over to check out Ann, proved it. "Just what I needed, icing on the cake of an already lousy day."

Jacob watched as Tommy turned onto the road and disappeared. He had graduated at sixteen and left home to earn his MBA. He'd been hired on with a million dollar company while still in college and climbed the ladder of success faster than anyone in the company's history. Jacob shook his head. A six figure income at the young age of twenty-four, no wonder Tommy changed.

Jacob knew life hadn't been easy for his friend. Tommy's father, Mr. Stevenson, was a hard man who demanded control. Tommy had originally tried to please him, but his strong spirit refused to be broken and he fled as soon as he could. Although he'd changed in many ways, Jacob knew he still had some good left in him. A younger sibling of Tommy's once mentioned a truck load of new furniture had been delivered to their mother, but their father refused it. Jacob was sure Tommy had only wanted his mother to have something nice. But his father probably saw it as a challenge to how he provided. Thus, the constant friction.

Jacob turned and saw Ann at the kitchen window. She concentrated on the dishes, unaware of her admirer. Jacob viewed her delicate features. She scowled at whatever was in her hands. Her lips were slightly drawn and a tendril of hair hung over one side of her face. Would Tommy show enough respect to leave her alone? He had driven all the way over to see what she looked like. He had entered Jacob's house without him, to be close to her. He had asked her out.

She was beautiful.

And Tommy knew it.

♡♡♡

The next day, Ann stepped into the kitchen feeling bright and cheerful. The coffee pot still sat empty. She carried it to the sink. As she reached for the faucet, a sigh sounded from the direction of the living room. She set the pot down and tiptoed around the table to peer into the adjoining room. Surprised, Jacob was still asleep on the sofa. He'd overslept. His late night hunt must have worn him out.

Thankful he was sound asleep, Ann crept closer to stare at her sleeping prince. His muscular thighs were wrapped in worn jeans and tangled in an old afghan. His broad chest, covered in a white t-shirt, rose with each peaceful intake of air. His hair lay in a soft mess of waves and thick dark stubble shadowed his jaw. One arm hung off the couch while his face turned into the elbow of the other. She had to control the urge to touch the mound of his bicep, brush his hair back in place, kiss his cheek.

What would it feel like to wake up to him each day surrounded by his love, protection, and trust? She didn't mean for the sigh to escape and wake him. But it did.

"Good morning," he said huskily. "I must have overslept."

"I - I'm sure you needed it," she stammered. "I'll make you some coffee."

Jacob smiled at her. Did the color of her cheeks match the warmth that seized her?

Ann fumbled with a coffee cup. Her feelings for this man were so strong she was greedily thankful he hadn't met the cougar. She feared what might happen if he did.

God, please keep Jacob safe. I can't stand the thought of him being out there. And help me to keep my trust in you.

Breakfast was a mixture of chaos and laughter. The children had more energy than usual which resulted in spilled orange juice and burnt toast. Ann took it all in stride as she mopped up the sticky floor.

"Uh, Ann, is our toast burning again?" Ethan looked over at the toaster where little swirls of smoke began to rise.

"No." Ann quickly popped the bread up. "They're just right." She took the slices of toast to the sink and scraped off the darkened areas. She applied a generous amount of jelly before laying a piece on each child's plate.

"Perfect. That looks delicious." Jacob acted like he would eat Emily's.

"No. This is mine."

Ann watched with gratitude as Emily ate her slightly burnt toast without complaint. "Thank you," she mouthed to Jacob. Ethan had already eaten most of his and jumped from his chair ready to run outside.

"Hey, look. Tommy's here." The door flung open and Ethan was gone.

"I'll have to tell him the hunt's been cancelled."

Ethan's crazy hound had taken off sometime that morning. Since they'd already proven it was pointless to hunt without a dog to help track, their hunt had to wait for the hound to return. Jacob walked to the door, followed by Emily and Luke.

Ann set the breakfast dishes in the sink and watched as Tommy stepped from his car. His movements held an artful grace that added to his refined masculinity. He appeared very high-society. If she didn't know better, Ann would never believe his roots traced him to the

Ozarks. He had perfected his articulate speech until all traces of the area were gone. He cast a glance toward the house and Ann's skin prickled. She looked at her arms and blinked. Surely, he was harmless. Besides, Jacob wouldn't let him touch her. The old fears that had vanished, threatened to return. She could hear part of his conversation with Jacob and Luke, as they discussed the fruitless hunt from last night before they entered the house.

"Do you always look this lovely in the morning, Miss Ann?"

Ann narrowed her eyes as she looked from Tommy to Jacob and back to Tommy. "Only when I wake up to this family."

Unperturbed, Tommy stepped to her side and let his body gently brush against her thigh and arm. "I could help you with these dishes." His voice was as smooth and polished as his intentions, but Ann had been down this road often enough before.

"No thanks, I'm done." She pivoted, tossed the towel onto the counter and joined the children in the other room, but paused long enough to see Jacob's heated look burn a hole straight through Tommy.

♡♡♡

With Sunday only three days away, Jacob was more comfortable with Ann going home. To his relief, so was Ann. Since the hound had yet to return, it took away the need to keep Ann at his home. He could convince her to stay and use the children's schooling as an excuse, but Jacob didn't want to harm her reputation. Though the storm and cougar incident couldn't be avoided, to ask her to continue to stay would only fuel the sure-to-come ill-founded rumors. Now, he would have to settle back into his regular farm routine until their weekend hunt.

Tommy had stopped by, just as promised. Jacob didn't like the constant attention he directed to Ann. If Tommy was so glad he'd finally moved on, the guy sure had a funny way of showing it, which is exactly why Jacob offered to take her home so early in the day. If Tommy hung around, he didn't want him anywhere around his Ann.

As the Garret's home came into view, Jacob let out a low whistle. "Wow." He drove over the paved private drive where hundred year old cedar trees boasted their survival. The Garret mansion stood out like a cloud upon green pastures. Its stately pillars climbed forever upward and wrapped completely around two sides of the house. The driveway looped to the other side where Jacob parked his truck underneath an arched canopy probably designed for carriages many years before. "I've never been up to the house. It's really something, isn't it?"

"It is. But I have to say, it lacks the charm of a log cabin. Would you like to see the inside?"

"Sure, if you don't think your uncle would mind."

Ann led him to the back of the house through the kitchen entrance. After they passed through a screened-in porch they stepped inside an enormous tiled room with hardwood cabinets that lined three walls and an island near the center.

"I, for one, could never keep something like this clean. The more room, the more mess I seem to make!" Ann laughed at herself.

"I believe that. But I also know that once you're finished in the kitchen, no one can tell you ever stepped a foot in it."

"Thank you. I'll take that as a compliment, and use it against my mom every time she moans when I walk into her kitchen!"

Jacob couldn't get over the space. He stared at the vaulted ceiling and then her. "Do they entertain a lot?"

"Just their church group, and of course we hold our family gatherings here. With all the space, we don't have to rent motel rooms." She grasped his hand. "Come on, I'll show you the parlor."

The parlor? He felt like he stepped back into time. Was Annie from a wealthy family? If so, did he have any right to ask her to submit to the life of a farmer's wife? He would never have this kind of money, nor would he ever see a need for it.

Ann's voice interrupted his thoughts, ". . . and this is what we call our family's hall of shame."

Jacob looked past the baby grand piano and saw that Ann stood before a hallway just off the parlor. He followed her lead and found himself in a narrow passage that must have originally been set aside for servants. All along the wall to his right was picture after picture of smiling faces of Ann's family. He peered closer to a very petite little girl in pig tails. Jacob had to smile.

Ann moved closer. "That's me. I'm the one they call, Runt."

As they moved farther down the hall, Jacob noticed in every picture of Ann, she was either with an animal or working around the farm.

"I can't help but notice a pattern with your pictures. You always seem to be with an animal."

"Yes, much to my mother's dismay. She could never get me to sit still for a photo unless I could hold something soft and cuddly." As though picturing the past, she added in a far-away voice, "I always felt more at home here."

Jacob hoped for a particular answer. "Why is that?"

"I grew up in the suburbs. And though it has its charms, I suppose, I always thought I should have been born in the country. Here at my uncle's I had the freedom to explore, help with the farm life, and basically run wild."

Her answer satisfied him. He didn't need to worry about the life he could offer her. Ann was genuine. No wonder his dad had nicknamed her, Sunshine, that's exactly what she brought to his heart.

Ann tilted her head at Jacob. "What are you thinking about?"

"You, and the effect you have on me."

Her mouth made a small circle shape Jacob couldn't resist. He took her in his arms and pressed his lips to hers. Would it always be like this? The tremble of her lips reflected his heart. Though inside he was already saying, "I love you," Jacob continued to keep his secret. He took a reluctant step back. "I'd better head home."

♡♡♡

That evening, Ann sat outside her uncle's porch and listened to the nightly serenade. The rain had brought with it an awakening. Since the passing of the storm, all that could be heard in the evenings were the songs of numerous spring peepers, each one trying to out-croak its neighbor. Though sometimes deafening, it also brought with it a peaceful reassurance of the continuation of life.

Jacob had explained that every spring was introduced by these tiny little frogs, soon to be followed by the sight of bluebirds and fawns. He made everything sound so lovely, it left a longing in Ann to want to belong here as well. To be familiar with all the changes the seasons offered in this little touch of Eden.

Ann stretched and opened her eyes. Friday morning, only two more days before she saw Jacob again. Jacob. She even enjoyed saying his name. Another thought hit her. She woke up peaceful. The last time she awakened here, it was from the nightmare that had haunted her sleep for months. She hadn't experienced any of them since she'd met Jacob.

"Wow! Love's a powerful thing." Ann jumped out of bed and joyfully went about her morning with a heart full of praise.

It amazed her how much she not only missed Jacob, but also everything tied to him. His amazing children. His father's loving smile. The warmth of his home. She couldn't wait until Sunday. She concentrated on doing as much as would keep her busy. When the phone rang she almost dropped the dish in her hand.

"Hello?"

"Ann, it's your mother." Her voice sailed across the wire as if there was no distance between them at all. "I'm not calling to talk but to inform." She paused as though to give her daughter time to prepare herself. "Janice has gone into premature labor and we're at the hospital now. I thought you might want to be here."

Ann's chest tightened with fear for her brother's wife. "I'll leave as soon as I can throw a bag together."

Chapter Eighteen

Ann hung the phone up after talking to her mother and realized she would need to get hold of Jacob. Her hometown was five or six hours away, depending on traffic, and driving to his house would be out of the question if she wanted to make it before nightfall. But since he lacked a phone, what choice did she have? Or, she could call the Stevenson's and ask them to relay a message to Jacob since she was certain he'd be stopping by to check on them. Ann slumped in a kitchen chair. Decisions like this shouldn't be so hard. She sat up straighter as a new idea came to mind. To keep the message from getting misquoted, she would leave a note for Jacob on the door. The Stevenson's could let him know to stop by and get it.

Relieved with her decision, Ann wrote the letter and called Jacob's neighbors.

"Hello," came a youthful voice.

"Hi, this is Ann—"

"Hi, Ann! How are you? You wouldn't believe how good Joseph is doing." The excitement came across the line in a loud whirl.

Ann smiled and listened as one of the little brothers told her everything he could think to say until someone finally took the phone from him. "Hello, this is Tommy Stevenson. May I help you?"

"Hi, Tommy, this is Ann. I have to leave town for a few days, and I wonder if you could let Jacob know to come by and get a note I plan to leave for him."

"For you, Ann, I'll do better than that. I'll come by right now and pick it up so he won't have to drive out." Without waiting for her response, Tommy said good bye and hung up.

"Okay," Ann said aloud to herself. "He must really need a break from his siblings."

Twenty minutes later, Tommy's voice sounded from the kitchen. Ann froze on the stairs, her shoulders tensed. Why was he in the house? Did she not hear him knock? She continued to drag her suitcase down the steps behind her, intent on meeting him where he was.

Too late. He appeared at the bottom of the stairs.

Ann stiffened on the bottom step, her skin prickled. He stood too close.

Tommy winked and leaned closer. "This works much better for us. I don't have nearly as far to bend down if I were to—"

Ann pushed him away and stomped toward the kitchen. "Haven't you heard of a door bell?"

He clicked his tongue. "Your aunt is a much better hostess."

Ann stopped and looked over her shoulder. "How would you know that?"

"She makes the best lemon tarts in the world. I let her know every time I'm home and she whips up a batch. Sorry if that bothers you. Forgive me?" Again, he not only invaded her space but blocked her exit.

Ann assumed her relatives knew Tommy from their annual community picnic. She chose to play it cool. "Of course. And I'm sure you won't mind being a gentleman and carry this to my car, would you?" She smiled and held the suitcase between them.

Tommy grazed his hand against hers before he accepted the luggage. "You don't honestly think you can get rid of me so easily, do you?" He stepped to the side and positioned his hand on the small of her back as they made their way to the kitchen. Ann struggled to hold onto her anger, as fear threatened to gain control.

Before they reached the door, Tommy stopped and turned her to face him. "Tell me the truth, are you running from the Neanderthal?"

Ann laughed in his face. "No. Actually, I'm about to be an aunt for the first time. I'm on my way home to where my sister-in-law is having the baby."

She picked the sealed envelope off the counter and handed it to Tommy. "Your reason for stopping by."

Tommy stared at her for a moment. "Yeah, about that . . ." He brought her hand to his lips and lightly kissed it.

Ann jerked back as though she'd been bit. She stepped backward and bumped into the cooking island centered in the kitchen.

Tommy narrowed his eyes. "It was just a kiss on the hand, Ann. Don't tell me you prefer a poor farmer's kisses?"

"You're jealous."

"Of, Jacob? Ha. I can have any woman I want."

"Except me."

Tommy stepped closer. "I'll be a millionaire in no time. I could give you anything you want."

Ann tried to step around him but his arms stopped her. "Tommy, let me go."

"We have the house to ourselves, no kids to interrupt, and you're telling me to let you go?"

Ann scowled. "Have you never been turned down before?" His arms dropped to his sides as though he finally caught on. "I'm not that kind of girl, Tommy. I'm not after your title, your wealth, or your body."

"Then what does a girl like you want?"

Ann sighed and thought of Jacob. "All the things you're not ready to offer or either can't."

"Such as?"

"Love. Security. Contentment . . . peace. That's just to name a few."

She turned and made it to the door. Before it could close, Tommy was beside her with the suitcase. She locked the house, thankful they were outside, and continued to her car.

Tommy's steps slowed behind her. "You're in search of peace, too?"

It was more than a question.

"I have peace that comes from Jesus. But what I meant is, it's important the person I choose to be with have that peace as well. You're lost, Tommy. Living to please yourself isn't attractive to someone like me."

"Hmm." Tommy shoved his hands in his pockets and stepped back as Ann got behind the wheel of her car. She rolled down the window before she shut the door.

"Thanks for taking my note to Jacob."

Tommy cleared his throat. Gone was the man and his search. Back was the suave, charmer Ann knew him by. He lowered himself to her window and in one fluid moment, his lips sealed over hers. Ann's breath stilled in her throat. She tried to jerk away but his hand pinned her head so she couldn't turn. He slowly peeled back and allowed his fingers to trail her cheek. "Think of me while you're gone."

Fury and shame colored Ann's cheeks. She shoved the transmission into drive and stomped the gas pedal. Gravel pinged as it hit the BMW. Whether it made contact with its owner was of little concern.

She'd only driven a mile when the dam broke. Tears slid down her face in rapid repetition. She blinked in an effort to see the road. Why hadn't she given him a piece of her mind? Why didn't she step from the car and slap his face? Had she lured him on, or given him the wrong idea?

An hour of driving passed before she accepted the truth. He had been in the wrong. There was no need to take back the burden of guilt.

Ann met her parents in the waiting room. They came together in a rush to exchange hugs and kisses. Concern etched the corners of Ann's eyes. "How's Janice and the baby?"

"They're taking the baby now, so say a prayer everyone will be all right. Bradley's staying with her, but he'll let us know something as soon as he can," her mother told her.

"I'm not surprised my brother's in there. He's been so excited to finally be a dad. I prayed for them nearly the whole way here." The other part of the trip she'd worried over Jacob.

Perhaps it wasn't a good idea to let Tommy take the note. She didn't want to put false ideas into Jacob's mind that Tommy had a chance with her. And, there was still the possibility he hadn't given the note to Jacob at all.

Would Jacob be thinking of her as much as she was of him? Did he miss her? Was he experiencing doubts or regrets? She never knew love could be such a whirlwind of emotions.

Ann's mother informed her of the latest information about her cousins while her father sat across from her silently watching, as if he knew something was different with his daughter.

He got up and stretched and waited for his wife to pause before he interrupted. "Okay, you've had your turn, now it's mine. How about it, Pumpkin, want to take a walk?"

"Sure, Dad." She smiled as she bent to kiss her mom's cheek. "We'll be back soon, Mom."

As they walked down the hall, Ann sensed her dad watching her again. His voice proved her right. "Are you going to tell me or do I have to play the guessing game?"

Ann sighed, "Dad, that was when I was little."

"Pumpkin, I hate to be the one to break it to you, but you're still little." He smiled at her playful frown and put his arm around her shoulders for a light squeeze.

"Don't remind me, I'm the runt of the McHaven's."

Her dad put a finger under her chin and raised her eyes to meet his. "But a runt with a stolen heart, would be my guess."

Ann stumbled at the truthfulness of her father's words. He guided her to a set of nearby chairs where she slumped into a seat. He then coaxed the entire story from her.

"And now that I'm here, I can't stop wondering. I feel so . . . well, like my feelings are out of my control. When I'm with him, I'm on cloud nine, but when he steps out the door my heart feels heavy with doubt wondering what he's feeling from one moment to the next."

She took another breath but still didn't straighten her shoulders. "And then sometimes, we can be within a foot of one another and just by one little thing he said or didn't say, I'm troubled all over again."

Having fully exerted herself, Ann collapsed against the chair and released a deep pent up sigh. With growing agitation at her father's silence, she opened her eyes and found him smiling.

"What on earth could you possibly find so humorous right now?"

"I was just wondering . . . when do I get to meet my future son-in-law?"

"Oh, Dad, this is serious!"

"Finally, there you are." Her mother rounded the corner a bit breathless. "Janice had a baby girl and they're both doing great. Come on, Bradley's waiting for us."

Ann's troubles flew to the back of her mind as the excitement of new life took center stage.

The weekend flew by in a flurry of family gatherings, all anxious to look at pictures of their new family member between visits to the hospital. Ann was thankful for such a close and supportive family. She caught herself wondering if Jacob's father was all he had to lean on during his personal trials.

Ann thought back to the support of not only her parents, but of her relatives after her latest job as a nanny. Everyone opened their doors to her with offers to stay. While they weren't all Christians, they were very close to one another and were always quick to help out. It was something Ann was so accustomed to she often took it for granted. However, after meeting the Stevenson's and her talk with Tommy, she remembered just how good she had it.

While everyone congregated around the buffet of food she and her mother had prepared, Ann's cousin, Natalie, grabbed her arm and whisked her to the hallway. "Spill it, Ann. Because I know you're keeping something from me."

Natalie was the closest thing to a best friend Ann ever had. Since they were the same age, they naturally spent their time together at every family event. Today was like any other as they stopped in the hallway to release secretive giggles.

Ann faked a serious sigh. "I should've known I wouldn't be able to keep anything from you."

"Ha, like you would even want to. You were just being typical sweet Ann by letting Janice have all the attention. But now it's your turn."

An unexpected relief washed over Ann as she told Natalie about everything that had happened. Admitting her love for Jacob lifted an enormous burden and brought a wide smile to her face.

Natalie threw her arms around Ann's neck. "I'm so happy for you. And, from the sounds of it, it's definitely the real thing. So don't worry, because I bet Jacob's counting the hours until you get back. Now, can I give you a bit of marital advice?"

"Natalie, I'm not even engaged. Have you listened at all to what I've said?"

"I know, I know. But I read this in a book before I married Jimmy and it was the best advice I could ever receive."

"Okay, tell me."

"If it's not worth a fight, leave it alone."

Ann frowned. "What are you talking about?"

"It's simple, if something bothers you that the other person did or does, think about it before you say anything. If it's not worth an argument, then just let it go. I know this works because Jimmy and I have been married for five years and we have yet to have our first fight."

"That's impressive. Thanks, Natalie. If it could give me half the happiness you two have, it's worth it." Ann gave her cousin a grateful hug. "I haven't told my mom, yet. So don't mention it around her. I want her to fully enjoy being a new grandma this weekend without any added distractions."

Natalie laughed. "You mean you don't want her planning your wedding already?"

Ann nodded in agreement. Her mother would mean well, but as her cousin stated, her enthusiasm would have her making plans before Ann even had a ring on her finger.

They returned to the buffet and as Ann was about to enjoy her plate of food, her mother called from the kitchen.

"Ann, someone's on the phone for you."

She raised her eyebrows at Natalie and rose to take it. Jacob didn't have her number, but still, Ann hoped in her heart it was him.

"Hello?"

"Ann, it's me, Tommy." After a slight pause, he continued. "Our conversation has been on my mind since you left and I wondered if you had time to talk."

"Okay. But how did you get this number?"

"I have a MBA, Ann. I've been trained how to think and get things done."

She wasn't satisfied with his answer, but curiosity drove her past it. And, if he was still upset, she didn't need to worry since she could talk to him by phone. "What did you want to know?"

"If you'll open the door, I'd be more than happy to tell you."

Chapter Nineteen

The telephone gave a dial tone as the doorbell rang in the front hall. Ann's hand went limp and the phone dropped to the floor. Was Tommy really here? At her parent's home?

A cyclone of commotion followed, all brought about by one visitor. The first to answer was her Aunt Sophie, who announced him as Ann's boyfriend. Ann's jaw slackened as she stumbled toward the foyer to quickly correct her aunt's error.

Her Uncle Pete saw her look of anguish and muttered something about Tommy being her ex-employer and he'd teach him a lesson the Navy way. When he was about to defend Ann with his fists her father came to the rescue and shooed everyone back to the buffet.

Ann stared at Tommy with narrowed eyes and shook her head. A thousand questions assaulted her mind.

"Are you okay, Ann?' her father asked.

"I'm fine, Dad . . . just confused."

"I take it this isn't my future son-in-law." He took her wide-eyed expression as agreement. "Call if you need me, hon."

After her father rejoined the others, Ann gave Tommy her full attention. He cast his eyes to the porch boards in a subdued manner. Ann hoped it wasn't an act. "Let's step outside."

Tommy looked across her shoulder. "Wow, that's some kind of gathering in there. I didn't know if I was going to be hugged or boxed."

"I know which one I would've cheered on." Ann ignored his hurt gaze. "That's my family. Don't bother asking, we'd be here all night if I tried to explain everyone." Ann sat down in a chair adjacent to him on the porch. A curtain fluttered in the window. She wouldn't have to worry about Tommy trying anything. Her protective family would keep him from that.

Ann looked pointedly at Tommy. "I think you have some explaining to do. Like why you're here and how did you find here?"

"I'll explain the first part. The second I'll keep you guessing." Tommy exhaled and ran his palms back and forth against his Armani clad legs. "I've had this awful tightening in my chest since we last spoke. I know you're a Christian like my parents, but I thought perhaps you would be easier to talk to than them.

"I'm aware I'm not living the way I should," he went on. "In fact, I think I've succeeded in living the exact opposite of how God would have me." Tommy looked out across the yard. He seemed to walk through his thoughts with care. "Nobody has ever talked to me in such plain terms before. I don't know if they were afraid they'd offend me or afraid of how I'd react. I know you didn't say much, but what you did say really got through to me and wouldn't leave. So here I am, in hopes you can release me of all the turmoil you instilled before you so mercilessly drove away."

"And the kiss?" Ann narrowed her gaze. "I'm still mad about that."

"Oh, yeah. The kiss." Tommy flexed his jaw. "I'm sorry. I was way out of line." A lengthened silence followed.

Ann reached for Tommy's hand. "If you want my help, it might help if you prayed with me. On my own, I can't help you. But I'll pray that through Jesus your eyes will be opened and you'll be blessed with understanding."

He looked from his feet to Ann. Fear and doubt were evident in his eyes. Ann squeezed his hand. "You don't have to pray your own prayer right now, Tommy. Just bow your head with me."

After he nodded in agreement, Ann prayed. "Lord, touch my mouth and put the words that You'd have me speak on my lips so that I may be a blessing to You and Tommy."

Ann hoped he would see how genuine she was and not think of her as another "religious" person. "My aunt taught me to memorize scripture and that one I tweaked into my own prayer. They can be really helpful."

"Ann, I was raised with the Bible shoved down my throat. I do know a thing or two." Tommy looked down at his hands before he softly spoke again. "I guess somewhere along the way, I just got lost."

For the next two hours, Ann battled Tommy's questions and uncertainties. She was amazed at how easily scripture came to mind. It had to be the work of the Lord. If God worked this hard to draw Tommy back, what awesome calling might He have set aside for him? But excited as she was by the prospect, it couldn't compare to the exhilaration that claimed her when Tommy admitted he was a sinner and needed the saving grace of Jesus.

She stressed the need to stay strong enough not to allow the material gains of this world to distract him and encouraged him to begin this new life-change by taking the focus off himself and serve others.

Through tears and grateful hugs they said their good byes. Ann's father joined her on the porch to wave as the BMW drove away.

"What was that all about?" Her father asked.

"King Solomon."

Her father raised his brows in question. "Care to explain that weird comment?"

"In Ecclesiastes, Solomon speaks of all that he gathered for himself. Vineyards, gardens, slaves, livestock, treasure, and of course that big harem he's so well known for." She returned her dad's smile at her light humor. "Yet, at the end, he says it was all meaningless, vanity and vexation of the spirit. Just like my friend Tommy, who should just pick up a towel."

"I followed you pretty good up until the towel part. Why pick up a towel?"

Ann shrugged her shoulders as if it was simple to understand. "Like Jesus. He washed his disciple's feet as an example that none of us are above serving others. King Solomon served himself and even with all of his riches he wound up miserable. So it goes without saying, we should all just pick up a towel." Satisfied with her logic, Ann moved to go back inside.

Her dad shook his head and smiled.

♡♡♡

Jacob wasn't at all impressed with the outcome of the day. Amateurs filled the hunt. They were more excited to see a cougar than admit the danger it posed. His aggravation toward Jim increased with each wasted hour.

"If it weren't for the kid and the dead cougar, Durham, I don't think I'd ever believe there was a cat out here. There's no trace of him anywhere." Jim exaggerated his point by waving his arm in an arch.

Jacob's chest expanded with air as he tried to control his annoyance. "Let's call it quits." He looked at the sloppy display of hunters and sighed. If there had been a trace of the cat, they would have marched over all the evidence by now.

Jim signaled to the others to end the hunt. Jacob hoped no one planned to stay for dinner. His mood couldn't tolerate their company. To add to his miserable thoughts, Tommy had announced Ann asked him to deliver the note.

Tommy's actions were a mystery. He'd previously made an open display of interest in Ann. Yet, when he delivered the letter he was subdued, as if something inside him admitted defeat. Aware of Tommy's history of radical mood swings, Jacob tried to not give it any thought. Though inwardly, he hoped Ann had made it clear she had no interest in him.

And what about Tommy's sudden announcement that he intended to head back home instead of stay for the hunt? Confusion muddled his thoughts even more. Tommy had been excited about the hunt, so, was he really headed home?

Jacob wished he had a phone. First thing come Monday morning, he'd have one installed.

The hunting crew packed up with tired apologies for their lack of success. With forced politeness, Jacob thanked them for their efforts and withdrew to the house. He enjoyed the solitude as he walked the short distance. Jacob wasn't one to often socialize and today had taken a toll on his tolerance level. Too many people. Too many voices. None of which belonged to the person he longed for most. He reached the door to his cabin. The children's enthusiasm over his arrival warmed his heart and lifted his mood.

Luke filled four bowls with hot chili as he eyed the scowl on Jacob's face. "Take a seat, Son. Some spicy chili ought to set things right."

Emily hurried to Jacob's side and tried to show him some books. "Daddy, I want you to read my books first. I only have three."

"After dinner, kitten." Jacob smiled at the little changes left by Ann. The children had never expected him to read a story every night. But since Ann's stay, they picked their books out early in the evening as though it had always been a family ritual. They also sang now. Whereas before, the only time he remembered hearing their voices in song was in the children's choir at church, now he heard them singing throughout the day. And if they didn't know the words to a tune, they simply hummed. It's often the little things in life that make a man feel rich.

Jacob took a seat with his family at the dinner table and waited for his father to say grace as usual. He lifted his head at his father's last words, ". . . and please keep Ann safe as You bring her back home to us. Amen."

He caught his dad's eyes before they were directed to the food. What was that twinkle for?

If he is hiding something, I'll never get it out of him. It was probably his open line to God. Jacob always admired the spiritual relationship his dad possessed. It was one he needed to get back to.

First things, first.

Ann.

♡♡♡

Though she had only confided in her father and Natalie, the rest of Ann's relatives sensed a change in her, too. They stated she was either too unsociable or daydreaming too much. Try as she might, she just couldn't stop her thoughts of Jacob and wondered if he wasn't doing the same.

Tommy's unexpected visit also added to the jumbled mess in her mind. The whole scene her family made was comical. It was a wonder any of them ever married, thinking how easy it would have been for their spouses to turn and run after their first introduction with the McHaven clan.

As the sun began it's descent on, yet another Saturday, Ann grew restless with anticipation toward leaving. Her mother asked if she would eat Sunday dinner with them. She paused to form her words so that she wouldn't hurt her mother's feelings, but her father stepped in.

"Ann has to be home for church tomorrow, dear. I believe there's going to be something special going on." He turned to Ann and winked, as though to assure her he'd kept quiet about what she'd shared with him.

Even with her father's help, Ann stayed until late evening. Every time she had an opening to leave, her mother would think of something else for her to do. Had her father stayed home, he would have stepped in for her. But he left to help Bradley set up the baby's room for her early arrival home.

Frustrated for not being strong enough to leave, Ann closed the door to her room in a depressed mood. Now she wouldn't be able to attend church with Jacob. Would he understand? Would he doubt her feelings for him?

Chapter Twenty

Ann looked around her old bedroom as frustration eased from her shoulders. Taped along the pale yellow walls were posters of horses and farm life. Having been born a country girl at heart, only to be chained to suburbia by birth, Ann found a way of escape through the pictures on her wall. How many hours were spent staring at them and daydreaming of a different lifestyle, she could never tell. Even the bottoms of the walls were decorated. Plastered right above the floor molding were cutouts of flowers and various gardens. It gave the illusion of being outside.

She often encouraged her mother to turn her room into something more useful since she'd left home. Now, she was thankful she hadn't. And to think, she was finally experiencing the very thing she'd always wanted. Her eyes grew heavy as she concentrated on the pictures until she could no longer keep them open.

Even before sunrise, Ann was awakened by somebody with admirable persistence. She willed herself to open her eyes and saw her dad stood beside the bed.

"What are you doing, Dad?"

"I figure if you leave within a half-hour, you should be able to make it to church on time."

Ann rubbed the sleep from her eyes with the back of her hand and replayed her dad's words in her mind. When they finally made sense, she jumped out of bed and threw her arms around him.

"Thank you, Dad! I'll be ready to go in fifteen minutes."

He chuckled softly. "Shhh, or your mom will wake up and you'll never get out of here in time. And, Pumpkin, don't get into too big of a hurry. I don't want you to get hurt out there on the road."

"I'll be careful."

Fifteen minutes later, Ann's father held out a travel mug of coffee. "You look as refreshing as spring. I'm sure I won't be the only one to notice."

Ann forced herself to be watchful of the speedometer. Excitement hummed through her. She wasn't going to miss church. In just a few short hours, she'd be back with Jacob. Back where she belonged.

♡♡♡

Jacob drove to Ann's alone Sunday morning. If she'd returned home, there wouldn't be enough room for all of them in the truck. And if she hadn't, he didn't want his disappointment to rub off on his children. Though her note didn't say whether she'd be back on Saturday or Sunday, he'd still driven out to the Garret's place yesterday, in hopes of finding her.

The vacant house had been a huge disappointment. Added to that, he still wrestled with guilt that she had to make the journey alone. Though she was a grown woman and more than capable, he continued to find reason to worry.

Jacob returned to the church alone. His children were already in their Sunday school classes. At least their hopes wouldn't be diminished, yet. He took a seat beside his dad and heard him say, "Don't worry, she'll be here."

Why couldn't he have inherited his father's faith? As the Sunday school hour ended and the children made their way to the pews, his question grated on his nerves even more.

More church members filed in and the greetings grew to a harmonious pitch, drowning out the nervous pounding of Jacob's heart. Ethan and Emily couldn't sit still and continued to turn back to see if Ann had walked in. Thanks to their grandpa, their hopes were still high. And if she doesn't make it? He didn't know when he would see her again. He didn't have her family's phone number; he was powerless in knowing how to contact her.

A quiet began to settle amongst the congregation. Jacob presumed the service was about to start and looked up from the tattered Bible he nervously rubbed. Everyone's attention focused on the glass entry doors behind him. He turned to look, and a delighted squeal emitted from Emily as she and Ethan ran to greet Ann.

She was a sight to behold. One he couldn't take his eyes off of. Like a soft spring flower emerging from a long winter, she took his breath away. As he rose to greet her, it took all his control to not run and whisk her up in his arms. He calmly walked to her side as she stood after hugging the children. Jacob gathered her hands in his and pulled her to him. With his head bent to hers he inhaled her scent, renewing a memory.

Ann looked at the small amount of space left in the pew. "Is there room?"

She peered up at Jacob and caught sight of a warm smile tug the corners of his mouth.

"I guess we'll have to sit really close," he said so only she could hear.

♡♡♡

Ann couldn't help but beam. At his light joking, all her tension drained away. He had missed her, and that was enough for now. Luke looked over from the other end of the pew and whispered, "Hello Sunshine, good to see you." Ann smiled back, her whole body filled with inexpressible contentment.

She was home.

Jacob rested his arm on the back of the pew behind Ann and drew her into the crook of his shoulder. She looked around and noted the church size to be around sixty members, which would explain the surprised looks she received when she first walked in. Hers was a new face in a crowd of people that had probably known one another for longer than she was old. As many of the members began to fill the choir, Ann looked up at Jacob.

"Did Tommy give you my note?"

Jacob hesitated. His eyes narrowed before answering. "Yeah. How's everyone doing?"

Ann quickly filled him in on her new niece before the choir began to sing. She was delighted to hear Jacob sing along. His baritone voice added a much needed balance to the overwhelming soprano in the front of the choir. She swallowed the giggle that wanted to follow. The lady was obviously proud of her voice and wasn't afraid to praise God with all she had. Ann followed suit and enjoyed the old hymns like never before as the words rang simple and true.

The pastor appeared eager, or perhaps it was nervous, to begin his sermon. He hardly waited for all the children to exit for children's church before he explained the necessity for his message. "The importance of purity is a subject often over-looked because of its sensitive nature, but important, none the less."

During the closing prayer, Ann went over his words in her mind. Could God have been talking to her and Jacob? Though not one to battle with lustful sins of the flesh, she had twice found herself in that very situation with Jacob. She'd taken an oath of purity as a young teen and determined to save herself for marriage. Now, however, she could understand why so many succumbed to the temptations of their flesh. Once allowed to step too far, it's much harder to deny a body of its desires. She could definitely see Satan's hand, or perhaps her own fleshly desires, leading her away from God's path.

In his message, the pastor mentioned Satan's plan of attack. "First, he wants to lure us away from God. By letting yourself get caught up in your own desires, you're less in tune to the voice of the Spirit." How right the pastor was.

But he hadn't stopped there. "Secondly, he wants to train us for divorce. Allowing sin to enter into a relationship before a covenant is made, is much the same as having a thorn in your side. Though you can still go on with life, it's constantly there, often causing pain and strife."

The pastor had finished with the final focus of his message. "And thirdly, Satan will rob us of hope."

Loss of hope. Ann was familiar enough with that feeling she never wanted it present in her marriage. And like the pastor said, "If it's a great marriage you're seeking, then the best way to plan for it is to preserve spiritual growth and purity today."

As the closing prayer was brought to an end, Ann stole a look at Jacob. He gave her a sly, sideways grin. One that said, "Yeah, I got it too." He gave her shoulder a squeeze before he stood and offered a hand to help her to her feet.

They made their way to the door, but everyone had waited for the opportunity to meet Ann. Jacob leaned near and said, "Might as well get this over with now." At a nervous nod from Ann, he stepped slightly behind her but kept a comforting hand on her shoulder, and allowed everyone a turn to greet her.

Ann couldn't recall receiving so many hugs in one setting. Even her large family wasn't this comfortable with one another. Not that it bothered her. It had quite an unexpected feel to it, as if spring now bubbled in her soul. Their love and affection had permeated the parts of her she'd allowed to become frozen for fear of being hurt again. They accepted her without question and were overjoyed she was with Jacob. As she repeatedly heard in whispers, "We always knew Jacob was a wonderful man, he just needed to meet his match."

When they were finally allowed to leave, thanks to Jacob's authoritative voice, the children danced delighted circles around their feet. Luke had waited for them outside. He turned to Ann. "Hey, Sunshine, good to have you home."

Jacob pulled Ann close as if in agreement. "Let's all go out to celebrate."

The restaurant he chose was a locally owned business that had been in the family since the town was settled. Pictures lined the walls of the local rural life, some dated back as far as the 1920's. Above them hung various objects of the townspeople's lives. To the right sat a canoe over the rafters with oars and a fisherman's net. Not far from that, hung an old Schwinn bicycle with a wide metal basket attached to the front handlebars. Ann was so lost in admiration she didn't realize Ethan had been talking about her.

"Can Ann stay with us again, Dad?" Ethan asked.

Jacob ruffled his son's hair. "She only stayed last time 'cause of the high water."

"But why can't she stay anyway? She could have my bed and I'll sleep on the couch."

Ann stepped in to help Jacob out. "Ethan, it isn't proper for adults to have sleepovers like kids do." Quickly moving the conversation onward, she added, "But I can come over and visit today."

Ethan accepted her answer without further questioning and ran to tell Emily who stood by a penny fountain.

The waitress brought their desserts to the table. What would it have been like to grow up in this town and waitress in a family owned business? *I bet she doesn't have to deal with nearly as many unmannered men as I did.*

In a town of less than three thousand, it was probably safe to walk to work during the daylight hours. Not that her hometown was awful, but since it had grown as fast as it did, it left behind many of the traits that lured people to small-town America.

Sharing her thoughts with Jacob and Luke, she asked, "I bet everyone here knows their neighbors and probably helps with barn raisings and such."

Luke's eyes crinkled at the corners. "You guessed right, Sunshine. Why, just last year at this time, we had a whopper of a storm blow through. It had a lot of mini tornadoes in it and tore the town apart, not so much the buildings, though, as the trees."

"But you'd never know it to look at the area now. Everybody pitched in to help clear the roads and mend fences. Even the roofers and loggers gave discounted prices for their work, since it was a natural disaster," Jacob added.

"I helped pull limbs." Emily sat proud and straight.

"You're not supposed to take credit for your good deed, Emily," Ethan corrected his sister, "that's what you get blessed for in Heaven."

Emily stuck out her bottom lip as the wheels in her mind turned. "I didn't get paid for it, so it's okay to tell."

Ann bit her lip to keep from smiling. "Regardless, all of you must have done a fine job. Your town looks very nice, Emily."

The corners of her mouth turned up in a grin. "Thanks, Miss Ann."

Once dinner was finished with dessert, Jacob drove back to the church parking lot and handed Ann her keys. "Thanks again for letting us use your car since we wouldn't all fit in the truck."

"You know I don't mind, but you shouldn't have filled the tank."

He smiled as he climbed out of the car and signaled for his kids to follow suit.

Ethan scrunched his face. "Ah, Dad, can't we ride home with Ann?"

"Oh, that would be fun. Can they?" Ann eagerly asked.

"I don't mind. And I'll have Grandpa to keep me company." He winked at his kids.

They returned to the cabin and the children ran off to change into play clothes. Jacob asked Ann, "Would you like to check calves with me?"

"Sure. Are we looking for new ones to tag?"

"That and making sure they're all still there."

"I'll grab my clothes from the car."

Jacob took hold of her elbow and steered her away from the door. "Tell me which bag it is and I'll get it."

"The blue one."

"The blue one it is, then. I'll be right back." He made his way out the door.

Ann smiled as Jacob strolled to her car. It was funny how she first pinned her rescuer as egotistical, and now, she'd fallen in love with him.

By the time the children had settled down enough to allow Ann to escape with Jacob, the evening sun began to set. As they crested a hill, Ann's breath rushed from her lungs at the beautiful display. Streaks of every shade of orange intermingled with hues of pink and purple spread across the horizon meeting with the green of the field. It brought to mind an image of God with a paintbrush in His hand. She could definitely get used to country life.

She turned to Jacob expecting to see her enjoyment mirrored on his face, but instead, heard his deep intake of air and felt his body tense next to her. She noted he paid extra attention to his driving. Had she done something wrong? Silence soon enveloped them, like it often had before her trip home. What had spurred this? She replayed scenes from the day. Then it dawned on her. Tommy. Before she could ask any questions of her own, Jacob's voice claimed the silence.

"So, how did Tommy get to be a messenger boy?"

Chapter Twenty-One

Ann answered Jacob as honestly as she could. "I didn't feel I had enough time to drive out here. I called the Stevenson's to let you know I'd leave a note for you on the door. Only, Tommy insisted on bringing it to you."

Jacob nodded his head in a slow yes and said nothing.

"There's something else you should know." Ann paused and hoped he was slow to anger and quick to understand. "Tommy showed up at my parent's house."

Jacob's foot slipped from the clutch as he turned toward Ann. The truck lurched forward. Ann caught herself with her wrists to keep from hitting her head again on the dash board.

"Sorry about that," Jacob said.

"That's okay; I'm beginning to get the hang of it." She smiled and rubbed her wrists.

"What was that rat doing there? How'd he even know where to find you?" In a more subdued tone, he added, "I guess you told him."

"No, no. It was nothing like that. I had no idea he would show up and I still don't know how he found me. This story actually has a happy ending."

"Well, I've heard enough already." He reached for the ignition. "I can take you back." His voice resonated defeat.

Ann quickly yanked the key from the ignition and hid it under her leg. "I have a few things to say, Mr. Durham, and you'll just have to get over taking me home, because I'm not backing down. Sound familiar?"

♡♡♡

Jacob couldn't control the smile that spread across his face. He loved Ann's spunk. He shifted his back toward the corner of the truck door and rubbed his chin, thankful his heart could resume its normal beat. "Okay, pretty lady, you've got my full attention."

After she caught him up on their conversation prior to her drive to her parent's home, Ann relayed her talk with Tommy on the front porch. "Did you know Tommy wasn't a Christian?"

"I knew he'd strayed from his raising." He placed his arm over her shoulders and drew Ann into a warm embrace. "Is it safe to assume you don't have any feelings for Tommy?"

"Even if I didn't have eyes for you, I still wouldn't have them for Tommy."

"Good, because I don't like the idea of sharing you." He shrugged and gave her a sheepish smile. Kissing her forehead he asked, "Why don't you like Tommy, just out of curiosity?"

"Because he's everything you're not."

Satisfied, Jacob stole a kiss before accepting the keys from Ann. Though he longed to continue kissing her, he started the truck forward. The morning's sermon was still fresh on his mind. Which is where he planned to keep it.

He kept a look out for calves. "We still haven't spotted number 32."

"What color is she?"

"He's a Hereford, so he'll be red with white down the back of his neck and a white face."

They'd driven a short distance when Ann shouted, "Oh, I think that's him. Over there." She pointed to the edge of the field.

Ann sighed and clasped her hands together. "Ah, thank the Lord. I was beginning to think my prayers for the little guy had been too late."

Jacob had grown accustomed to her constant referral to God and prayer. The similarities between Ann's faith and his mother's touched him. Who'd have thought God would bring the perfect woman to him with the flood?

Jacob pointed to the side of the field. "Looks like we've got some fence to mend."

Ann's gaze followed Jacob's to where a tree had blown down over the fence during the storm. "I thought you'd checked it all."

"I did. But with the saturated ground and the strong winds, it must've fallen afterwards."

They stepped from the truck and walked over to survey the damage. "I'll have to bring my chainsaw back to cut the tree up. Hopefully the cattle have the good sense to stay inside the fence." He studied Ann for a moment. "Do you feel like fixing fence this evening?"

"Really, you want me to help you?" Ann's enthusiasm bubbled through her voice.

"It's already getting late and I could use an extra hand. Dad won't mind staying with the kids." He held her hand as they walked back to the truck. "It might be a good idea for you to see what farm life entails."

While Jacob collected the gear they would need, Ann stepped inside to tell Luke and the children their plans. Instead, she found Luke with his leg propped up with a bag of frozen peas on his ankle.

Ann knelt by his chair, her brow wrinkled in concern. "What happened?"

"Nothing to get upset over, Sunshine, I just tripped in a hole." He shifted in the chair and added, "I'm not sure if it was a gopher hole or an Ethan and Emily hole. Either way, what's been done is done."

Ann removed the ice and checked Luke's ankle. "I don't think it's broken, but it is a bad sprain. You'll have to stay off it for a while."

Jacob stepped through the door. "Ann, what's the hold up?"

"You're dad hurt his ankle."

Jacob met Ann beside his dad as she filled him in on what happened. After he took a look at Luke's ankle, Jacob took purposeful steps down the hall to where the children quietly waited in their rooms. He stood in their doorway. Long, sad faces revealed their guilt.

"I'm sorry, Dad."

"Me too, Daddy," Emily added.

"Thankfully, Grandpa's ankle isn't broken, but you've both lost your digging rights. You're not to handle the shovels unless told to. Understood?"

"Yes, Dad," they both answered.

"Ann and I have to mend fence. You two be on your best behavior and take good care of Grandpa and Candy."

"Okay," they both replied.

♡♡♡

Jacob sawed while Ann pulled away limbs. Next, they stretched new barb wire then walked the fence line where it wound its way through the woods to check for more fallen trees.

"Jacob, it's getting dark, let's turn back."

"You're right. I keep peering through to the field and figure we have more time, but it gets awful dark here in the trees."

Leaves crunched.

Jacob turned toward the sound. Nothing but shadows. An eerie sensation spread across his shoulders like crawling spiders. He clasped Ann's hand in his. "Let's go."

As they traced their steps toward the truck, Jacob heard the near-silent foot falls of something keeping pace. He pulled Ann to a stop and motioned to be quiet with a finger against his lips. Ann's foot settled on the ground. Their tracker did the same. Ann's eyes widened as she looked up at Jacob. He motioned his head forward. They gained a few yards before stopping again. Just like before, as they took their last step, their stalker stopped.

In a more determined trot, they headed for the truck. Neither of them spoke. They were almost free of the woods. The safety of the vehicle within sight.

Then, the mountain lion released a blood curdling cry.

Ann screamed in response. Jacob squeezed her hand as he broke into a full run.

They reached the truck and Ann sailed across the seat. He came in behind her and slammed the door. His rifle hung in the window, but the increasing darkness would be as much a foe to him as the cougar. Ann's hands trembled in her lap, she needed the security of the house. He started the engine and hurried back through the field.

Jacob parked the truck in the lean-to and helped Ann down from the cab. "We're safe now." He pulled her to him in a warm embrace. She clung to him like a life line.

"You did good, Annie." He rubbed her back before he looked into her eyes. "You okay to go in with the kids now?"

Ann blew a steady breath from her lips. "Yeah. The walk to the house will help, too."

At the cabin, nothing was mentioned about their experience until the children were nestled in their beds. Ann agreed to read them a story before she joined the two men already at the table with a cup of coffee waiting for her.

She sat down and clasped the warm cup with both hands. Jacob glided his hand across the back of her shoulders. "Are you all right? You still look pale." He reached over with his other hand and placed it on her arm. "Ann, you're freezing!"

"I'll be fine," she chattered. "I should head home."

Jacob shot Luke a perplexed look before he realized Ann's body was fighting off shock. He slid his chair back, scooped Ann up in his arms and carried her to his bedroom. She didn't even protest. He laid her on the bed and searched for wool socks to pull over her feet. Then covered her with a layer of blankets.

"I want you to rest, Annie, while we handle the worrying." He kissed her forehead and said nothing of her state of shock. He didn't want her to worry over anything else.

"Jacob," Ann whispered as she reached for his hand. She pulled it to her and closed her eyes, asleep within seconds.

Fear and guilt washed over him as he continued to stare at Ann's whitened face. Outraged with himself for the danger he'd exposed her to, he stood with the determination of David meeting Goliath. He strode into the room where Luke sat with his foot propped and laid out plans with his father.

♡♡♡

Luke stayed over and slept in the recliner while Jacob wrestled with sleep on the couch. He rose earlier than needed and crept into his bedroom to check on Ann, just as he had done countless times during the night. Her cheeks were rosy from warmth the blankets offered and she still slept soundly.

Luke stirred in the recliner as Jacob reentered the living room. "She'll be fine, Son. We'll help each other out today." He smiled and motioned to his foot.

"How's your ankle?" Jacob walked over. The swelling had gone down a little, but it was still too sore for Luke to move it.

"It'll heal. But if you want to keep to the plan, you'd better head out before Sunshine wakes up."

Jacob nodded. He didn't know how Ann would take his hunting the cat alone, but he had no other choice. Tommy wasn't an option. As far as Jacob knew, he'd returned home, and the conservationist and his hunting team,well, he'd probably do better on his own. With Luke's ankle injured, it only supported the fact. Not wanting to waste any time, he hastily readied himself and Trigger before riding out with Ethan's hound in the lead.

♡♡♡

Ann woke up confused. She could barely move beneath the pile of blankets, and she didn't recognize the room. She looked around and remembered the closet where Jacob retrieved the sweater. On the adjacent wall was the small window that now filtered in shafts of sunlight. She struggled to clear her mind and realized why she was there. Ann sat up in bed. She must have slept through most of the morning. Why then did she feel so groggy?

She stumbled out of bed and headed for the kitchen, following the smell of coffee that beckoned her to start the day. "Good morning, Luke." She grabbed a cup.

He hobbled with old crutches and made his way to the table. "How are you feeling this morning?"

"Weird," she chuckled, "but alive." She took a seat beside him. "Is Jacob feeding cows?" Luke directed his gaze to the floor. Ann's heart paused. It only supported the hesitant feeling she'd awakened to. She forced herself to breath deeper as Luke explained Jacob's decision to hunt alone. Dread weighed heavy on her soul, as though some unforeseen event threatened to change their lives forever.

Ann contemplated taking a walk in the yard to pray but Luke interrupted her thoughts. "I can probably find another sweat suit for you if you need it."

She viewed her rumpled clothing from the day before. "It's okay. I have clothes with me. I came straight from my parents to church, yesterday. I'll go outside to grab the rest of my stuff."

Ann excused herself and stepped outdoors, appreciating the blast of cool spring air. As she walked to her car, she remembered the verse Jacob quoted just days ago. Fear not, for thou art with thee. She quoted the rest to herself and found comfort in God's word. Please God, watch over Jacob and keep him safe in Your care. Help me put my trust in You and not give in to worry and fear.

The children would soon awake. She retrieved her bag and returned to the house. Upon opening the door, two energetic children ran to hug her good morning.

♡♡♡

Moses led Jacob and Trigger further into the back country where rolling farmland gave way to high ridges and menacing outcrops of rock. Jacob was more than thankful for his horse. Cougars were capable of covering 20 miles in a given day.

Pink granite boulders decorated the hillsides; sometimes rising as much as fifty feet toward the sky. Jacob had stopped counting at seven miles. They were much farther by now. The landscape was so dissimilar to anything on the farm; he assumed they had crossed well over onto state ground.

His thoughts drifted home. How was Ann feeling and how had she taken the news of his hunting alone? He'd hoped the hunt would be over by now. His time with Ann had been too disrupted to fully enjoy.

With growing aggravation, he noted the beginning shadows of late afternoon. This would give unfair advantage to his adversary. Trigger stumbled on loose shale and snorted with disgust while he regained his footing. Jacob accepted the fact he wouldn't get back anytime soon and forced his attention to the job at hand.

He yawned, rubbed the back of his neck and wished for another cup of coffee. Then it happened. The baying he'd been waiting for. He nudged his heels into Trigger's flanks and blazed a path toward the hound's excited voice. They caught up with him at the creek's edge. "Come on boy, sniff him out," Jacob encouraged as he pulled his Sharps from its sheath.

Moments after he crossed, Moses again caught the cat's scent and took off. Jacob followed an eerie feeling and looked up. The cat stood below a high ridge. Its golden coat boasted a healthy sheen which only helped highlight its excellent, muscular build. It appeared oddly calm, as though it held no concern for the canine closing in on its trail.

A cold sensation traveled up Jacob's spine as the cougar stared straight through him.

Chapter Twenty-Two

Jacob watched with amazement as the cat turned and leaped fifteen feet straight to the top of the cliff. While Moses bayed and tried to claw his way up the bluff, the cougar slipped behind a boulder out of sight. Jacob groaned at the missed shot. Now that he had a good look, he promised himself it wouldn't happen twice.

They'd lose precious time going around the bluff, but Jacob didn't know of any other way. With haste, they worked their way around and paused as they approached the spot where the cat had perched. Trigger blew nervously and shook his head. Jacob would have to dismount at some point. Trying to pull off a successful shot on a spooked horse would be a waste of time.

He encouraged the gelding onward until they reached the top. Moses had his nose to the ground. Was he confused? Jacob watched him scan the area back and forth in nervous abandonment as he tried to locate their enemy.

Jacob shifted uneasily in the saddle. He was completely outside of his comfort zone. But it was now or never. He dismounted and began to secure his ride to a nearby sapling.

In a blur of motion, Moses lunged toward a crevice in the rock before he scrambled backward in sheer panic followed by an angry assailant. It was on top of the dog before Jacob could react. Drawing in a quick, but steadying breath, Jacob positioned his 45-70 to his shoulder and waited for his opportunity. It didn't take long. The enraged feline hovered over the helpless hound and gave way to perfect aim. Just as he squeezed the trigger, the cat sensed his presence and leaped into the air. It cleared 20 feet before disappearing into the forest. At the same time as the rifle blast, Trigger reared back and emitted a high pitched whinny that sounded more like a scream. His round eyes were huge as he broke free and bounded down the trail.

In a desperate attempt to contain his anger, Jacob clamped his jaw shut and turned his attention from horse to dog. He could barely make out the back end as the canine raced after the cat. Jacob threw his head back. "Errr! Can anything else go wrong?"

Not far into the forest he made out a trace of blood. Was it the dog's or had he managed to wound the cat? He hoped for the latter and continued with caution, following the scant trail the best he could. Now and then, more drops reassured him he was still headed in the right direction.

With lengthened shadows, the beginning presence of evening made itself known. How long had he been traipsing around in here? And how far into the forest had he gone? I hope I can still find my way out when this nightmare is over.

Just as Jacob thought his efforts were in vain, movement about ten yards to his right grabbed his attention. He slowly let out the breath he'd unconsciously held and hunkered down.

Time stalled. His knees grew stiff. What was going on? Where was the cat? And what of Ethan's addle-brained dog? As Jacob started to rise, a limb snapped from behind. The hairs on the back of his neck rose.

He spun his rifle around. A distant haze taunted him, followed by eerie silence. Beads of perspiration formed along his hairline. Every sound intensified, as did the pounding of his heart.

A shrill whinny broke the silence then quickly stopped. Something rapidly approached. Jacob readied his rifle, unaware of what the shadows would reveal.

Every muscle tensed as he waited. Moments turned into hours until he thought he would explode from anticipation.

Branches broke and leaves crunched as Moses broke forth from the underbrush and collided into Jacob's chest.

"I swear dog if that cat doesn't put an end to you, I just might!"

Moses dropped himself against Jacob's leg and panted with exhaustion. Jacob tried to form a plan, but without his horse his vulnerable state robbed him of clear thought. He was in the cougar's domain, miles from civilization, with an undependable mutt and deserted by his horse. Jacob rose. An uneasy feeling still lingered in the air. Beside him, the hound began to whimper.

♡♡♡

The children sat beside Ann as she read. She tried to keep her mind on the story but her thoughts continually went back to Jacob. She lifted her head and stared at the window.

"Keep reading." Emily shook Ann's arm.

Thoughtful, she slowly turned to look at both children. "I think we should pray." She saw the questioning look in Ethan's eyes and stressed, "Right now."

Without hesitation, both children slipped from the couch to their knees. Ann knelt beside them and led them in a prayer for Jacob's safety. Afterward, she rose and turned to the family Bible instead of the children's book. It opened easily, its binding having been worn from generations of use. Ann let the pages fall freely, stopping when she noticed a highlighted verse.

Out loud, she read from Psalms. "The eyes of the Lord are upon the righteous and His ears are open unto their cry." Her eyes trailed to the next highlight. "The righteous cry and the Lord heareth, and delivereth them out of all their troubles." She saw the silent questions from the trustful children and knew she needed to be careful not to fill them with fear.

"Don't be afraid."

Ethan eyed her with wisdom beyond his years. "Is Dad in trouble? Is he hurt?"

She fought to keep her eyes from filling with tears. "I don't know, honey. But the Holy Spirit leads people to pray for those in need. And your dad was laid on my heart, so I thought it would be best if we prayed for him."

"Maybe he's cryin' like the Bible said," Emily offered.

Ann wanted to direct their thoughts away from the possibility of Jacob being hurt, though in her heart that's what she feared as well. "Perhaps he just needs help finding that 'ole ornery cat."

"Then we best pray that he finds it." Emily bobbed her head up and down as she spoke.

Ann smiled at Emily's comment. As the child prayed out loud, her thoughts went to the heaviness of her heart. It was then she realized the reason for her burden.

She was truly in love.

If given the chance, she would tell Jacob as soon as she saw him.

♡♡♡

Jacob peered into the darkened forest and strained to make out what his senses told him was there. Somewhere close the cat lurked. He had to be ready when it came into sight. Beside him, the hound bristled and bared his teeth. Jacob followed the dog and warily stalked ahead. He kept his eyes sharp and looked for the slightest movement.

Snap! The sound of the steel trap reverberated throughout the forest along with the hound's anguished cries. Jacob clenched his jaw shut with gritted teeth and choked back angry words. He knelt down and took note of the aged apparatus. He swallowed his frustration and spoke softly to the dog. Jacob kept his head up and allowed his eyes to steal glances at the trap.

The cat moved in with experienced stealth, seizing his opportunity.

Jacob locked eyes with it. The cat stalled. It swished its tail back and forth. Jacob drew his Sharps to his shoulder and waited for a clear shot. The cat purposefully weaved between trees, masking a clean shot to his nefarious heart.

Even with the darkened interior of the forest, Jacob could make out a smear on the cat's left shoulder. He did hit it with his earlier shot. The lion silently padded to his left. Jacob knew his life depended on keeping up.

He turned with the lion, careful to keep their eyes locked.

Frustrated, the cat twice changed direction and tried to come up from behind. Jim had filled him in on the hunting traits of a cougar; so far, the cat reacted just as predicted. Strangely, it was his next move that caught Jacob by surprise.

Without warning, the cat turned and bounded into the forest. "Crazy cat!" Jacob yelled aloud. "Stay put," he absently ordered the dog, as if it had a choice. With his only thought being the need to end the hunt and soon, Jacob ran in the direction of the feline.

Several yards deeper into the forest, Jacob came to a halt. It was too quiet. A shiver raced up his spine and gave him an unsettling feeling. Then the sound. A low growl, barely audible. Where had it come from?

He'd raced head-long into a trap.

He spun around to look behind him. Nothing. He tightened his grip on his rifle, every muscle tensed.

Leaves rustled above.

Jacob turned back and jerked his head up. He caught sight of the cougar's reflective eyes just before it flung itself through the air and landed on his chest. The impact of its weight knocked the rifle from his hand. The hard ground expelled his lungs of air. Jacob gasped for breath beneath the enormous beast. Giant paws swung at his face. He brought his forearms up to guard his eyes against the brutal attack. Struggling for his life, he swung at the cat with all his might, his only thought being survival. Undeterred, the enraged feline continued to battle for an opening to Jacob's throat.

Pain burned where his foe's razor sharp teeth made contact with his forearms. He was no match for the cat. Any moment, his next breath could be his last. His thoughts went to his family and settled on Ann. A love for a woman like he'd never known before secured his heart.

He had to live.

Jacob made a desperate last attempt. While the cat spat and clawed in a maddening rage, Jacob fought to draw his knees underneath his foe. He shoved his feet against the cat's belly. With all the strength he had, Jacob thrust his legs skyward and flung the cat to the side.

As they both scurried to their feet, Jacob dove to retrieve his rifle. Oblivious to any pain, he slid on the ground. In one fluid motion he'd regained his stance with his gun aimed.

Out of the blackness, Trigger appeared and reared back. His whinny sounded like a battle cry. With the strength of an army, he crashed down on the lion. As he raised his front hooves to repeat the motion, the cat snarled and lurched to the side to save itself from being crushed.

Jacob spun around. He sought for it through the trees.

Nothing.

Pure unadulterated fear ripped through his chest. Sweat and blood trickled into his eyes and burned. His vision blurred. The only audible sound was his breathing. Slowly, he made out the dog in the trap. His horse pranced with fright. It snorted and brought Jacob out of his daze. He blinked away the sweat and focused on the dog. It had probably been whimpering for a while, he just hadn't heard it.

A thickened silence enveloped the trio. Unnerving, it made things feel surreal.

As he knelt down to release the trap, Jacob tried to soothe the dog's nerves as much as his own and kept his voice calm. The hound worriedly licked Jacob's numerous gashes as his foot was freed. They limped side by side, while Trigger pushed for the lead. With watchful eyes, they retreated from the woods without so much as a snarl from the cougar.

They reached the bottom of the ridge and paused at the creek to quench their thirst. Once fully hydrated, the injured hound collapsed on the bank. His side heaved as he lay panting. Jacob cupped water to his mouth. He grimaced as pain seared through his entire upper body. Aside from his numerous cuts and bruises, several ribs felt cracked.

He brought a hand to his face and found a swollen gash just in front of his ear where the cougar's claws made contact. Thankfully, it missed his eye. With a grunt he stood, refusing to survey any more of his damaged body. If he was going to make it home tonight, he couldn't give in to the fear and knowledge of how injured he might be.

Jacob limped to his horse. "Be patient, this may take a while." He groaned as he pulled himself onto the saddle. He closed his eyes against the wave of pain that washed over him. The cold evening air invigorated him as he tilted his head back and sucked it in. He stared at the heavens. The sun had set exposing a few twinkling stars.

Surrounded by calm, he remembered the verse that sprang to mind while he battled in the woods. The eyes of the Lord are upon the righteous, and His ears are open unto their cry.

"God," Jacob prayed, "thank You for bringing me out alive. I sure don't feel righteous. Forgive me for turning my back on You for so long. I've been selfish and ignorant thinking I didn't need you. Any excuse I could come up with is useless since nothing is hidden from You. Please guide me back to You and safely home."

With a click of his tongue, Jacob steered Trigger to the edge of the woods. The moon began to reflect its fullness which eased the burden of their journey. Thankful for something finally turning out right, Jacob relieved some of the tension in his shoulders, but kept his eyes alert.

He sensed the cat's presence before he saw it, a silent form slinking along the edge of the field. He'd assumed it was further injured by Trigger's attack, yet watching it now, he couldn't believe how easily the cougar moved.

His anger increased with each breath. Jacob coaxed his mount closer and hoped for a clear shot. His heart pounded inside his chest. After only a few yards, he realized it was now or never.

With God-given strength he drew his rifle into position and readied his aim. He switched the safety to its off position and curled his finger around the trigger. He appreciated the feel of cold steel beneath his skin. Just as the cat attempted a leap to safety, Jacob squeezed the trigger. A resounding blast reverberated throughout the field and forest. The cougar's body fell with a muted thump to the ground, an end to its hellish existence.

Amazed his horse hadn't thrown him, Jacob patted the side of his neck and nudged him forward. He pulled Trigger to a halt, only yards from their prey and cautiously dismounted.

Armed and ready, he approached the still lion and picked up a long limb that lay nearby. He prodded the beast and heaved a sigh of relief. Their war had finally come to an end.

With the release of fear also came utter exhaustion. His knees weakened and threatened to buckle beneath him. Jacob turned to Trigger. He walked back and found his son's hound had summoned enough strength to catch up with them. He took pity on the brave critter and picked him up with what strength remained. He steadied the hound's length behind the saddle before painfully mounting.

Jacob continued toward home. Although he was eager to return to the farm, after an hour in the saddle, he could no longer hold on. The accumulation of his injuries and loss of blood left him sapped of strength. Twice, he caught himself before falling from his horse. Jacob slid his exhausted frame to the ground. He stumbled a short distance beside Trigger before he finally collapsed on the dew laden field.

Chapter Twenty-Three

Ann glanced out the window again. Still no sign of Jacob. A kitchen chair scraped against the floor. Ethan seated himself at the table, a replica of his father. She turned away again as fear for Jacob overwhelmed her. Why was she feeling this way? The dread that she'd awaken to had only increased as the day wore on.

"God, I can't let the children sense my fear. Please take it from me and bring Jacob home safely." Ann whispered her prayer before she served the family dinner.

She shoved her food around on her plate. Her stomach had turned into a solid weight. When everyone finished, Ann eagerly cleared the table, anxious for the work that would keep her hands busy.

It was Luke who gave her the push she needed. "Kids, I want you to go in your rooms and fold the clothes Ann washed." After they left, he hobbled into the kitchen and put an aged hand over Ann's. "The kitchen is clean, Ann. You need to stop all this fussing and do what really needs done."

Her eyes widened at Luke before her gaze turned inquisitive. Afraid to breathe the words, Luke said them for her. "Go. Bring our boy home, and tell him to stop worrying his old dad."

Ann threw her arms around him and hugged Luke, careful not to topple him from his crutches. Her throat thick with tears, she said, "Be praying for him."

"You mean continue praying for him."

Ann wasn't sure where to look; she just knew the feeling in her gut told her something was amiss, and Luke's words confirmed it. She grabbed the keys off the counter before she ran to the truck. Perhaps by the time she got it started she'd have an idea of where to begin.

The lonely dirt road was more desolate than usual. Long shadows cast by the full moon taunted her with the likeness of Jacob and Trigger. Ann rolled down both windows in hopes of hearing the horse give away their location. But all that answered was the sound of the truck's tires turning over gravel.

Ann continued to drive until her intuition guided her to a gate on her left. Trusting God was the one in control, she pulled the truck onto the overgrown driveway. She jumped from the cab and ran to unlatch the gate, anxiety building with each moment that passed. Its rusty hinges made it difficult to move. Ann lifted the weight off the front as she dragged it over to the side. Reluctantly, she paused to close it after she passed through and tried to make up for the time as she sped through the field.

The truck crested the top of a hill and Ann braked. Leaning out her window to whistle for Trigger, she could only hear the rumble of the engine. She switched off the ignition and climbed out of the cab. How could she possibly know which direction to go? But God had led her thus far.

She whistled again.

A faint whinny sounded from the far side of the field. Ann's heart leaped within her chest. "Jesus, please let Jacob be all right. I can't stand to lose him, not when I just realized how much I need him."

Back in the truck, she bounced through the field until she saw the outline of a horse. Her headlights also reflected a body crumpled on the ground.

"Oh, no!" she screamed, as she gunned the truck in their direction, breaking for an abrupt stop only yards away.

Ann slammed on the brakes and jumped from the cab. She hurried over to Jacob and fell on her knees. "Jacob! Jacob! You have to answer me. Jesus, please let him answer me. Ja—"

Jacob's hoarse whisper cut her off. "I've been trying to answer you, but you won't be quiet long enough to hear me."

Ann wiped her tears. "Thank you, God." She touched his cheek and he flinched as her fingers came close to the gash. "You look awful, can you stand?"

"Of course, I was just taking a breather."

Through the light provided by the truck, Ann saw the dark stains covering most of Jacob's upper torso. Her eyes darted around with a nervous tension. "I think you've lost a lot of blood. Let's get you in the truck before that lion comes back."

Jacob released a moan as he struggled to get up. "It won't be back. I shot it." Ann was still too nervous to let the news sink in. She pulled him to his feet and let the bulk of his weight lean against Trigger as she supported him around the waist. Trigger more than proved his worth, as he obligingly accepted the task. Ann reached for the reins and guided all three of them to the cab. Once Jacob was inside, she gently laid the dog in the bed of the truck before heading for the road, with Trigger close behind.

"Don't go to sleep, Jacob." Ann nervously patted his thigh and tried to hold herself together.

His eyes were closed, but his mouth revealed the slightest smile. "I don't have a concussion, just some cuts."

His voice slurred.

Panic rose in her voice. "You stay awake, Jacob Durham, you hear me? I didn't come all this way to lose you now!" A sputtered sob hitched her breath and shook her shoulders.

"Crying won't help me, Annie. Ask me questions," he mumbled.

"How old were you when Ethan was born?"

"Twenty-one, I think."

"Good. Okay, how long have you had Trigger?" When he didn't answer immediately, Ann shouted the question again.

"Stop yelling, Annie." His light chuckle was meant to ease her tension. "I'm thinking."

"You have to be quicker with your answers. I'm not very good in crisis situations."

"So I've noticed." His voice was barely audible now.

"Jacob, please stay awake. I love you, Jacob. I can't bear to lose you." Tears streamed down her face.

It was the slightest movement, but there against her thigh, Jacob moved his hand to touch her. She glanced down to see his bloody, swollen arm trying to comfort her. A sob escaped her throat. She turned to Jacob and saw a single tear fall from his eye.

"I love you, too." His words, though quiet and slurred, spoke volumes to her heart.

Ann sniffed and blinked rapidly. "You're going to be okay. I'll get you to a doctor." She turned to hide her fear. He'd lost so much blood.

Would he be okay?

Ann made it through the gate after opening it, this time she didn't bother to close it. She stopped long enough to lead Trigger in the direction of home then slapped his rump to get him going. She hated the thought of leaving Luke to worry, but didn't want to waste any time going the opposite direction from the hospital. She'd have to trust God to comfort them until she could call.

♡♡♡

Ann sat in the hospital waiting room with Emily on her lap and Ethan and Luke close by. She wore a pink sweatshirt Luke brought for her. After contacting the Stevenson's, she'd told them she wasn't fit for the children to see.

Jacob's blood stained her shirt.

Ann's legs were crossed and her foot continually tapped in the air. A warm hand reached over and covered her arm.

"Ann," Luke's voice was gentle and sad. "Why don't you find us a cup of coffee?" His loving eyes couldn't hide his own pain, yet, his thoughts were on her.

Touched by his thoughtfulness, Ann nodded. She needed to walk and pray.

Ann found her way to the chapel. She entered with hopes of finding solace, but it was already occupied by a couple. The disappointment that niggled her was pushed aside by guilt. *"Where three or more are gathered, there am I also . . ."*

She approached the couple and knelt beside them. After exchanged concerns, they spent the next few moments in prayer.

Their heads lifted and revealed swollen eyes and utter exhaustion. Ann's heart ached for their pain. She placed a hand over the woman's. The lady couldn't have been much older than Ann.

Her mouth turned down as she began to weep.

Uncontrolled tears rolled down Ann's cheeks as well. This couple's pain was so great she didn't give thought to her own.

"Dear God in Heaven," Ann began, "Please lend healing to our loved ones, strength to endure what's ahead, and acceptance for what we cannot change. And please, I ask you to comfort us in the midst of our trials. Amen."

The man pulled a handkerchief from his back pocket and wiped his eyes. "Thank you," he said as he stood. "We needed another's prayers. More than you could know."

"Yes," said the woman, "you said what I couldn't."

Ann watched them exit from the chapel. The man wrapped his arm around the woman. Her strength. Her protector.

She took a deep breath, grabbed a tissue from a box on the floor and dried her eyes. She'd have to rely on her prayer for strength to endure what she'd soon find out.

Ann walked toward the waiting room with candy bars in her pocket, two cups of coffee and hope in her heart. Luke's eyes lit up when they met hers.

"Good news!"

Before Luke could say more, the children filled Ann in. Tears pooled in her eyes as bits and pieces of their conversation made sense. "Loss of blood. Sixty-Two stitches. Cracked ribs. Daddy's coming home tomorrow!"

Luke directed Ann to a nurse that showed her to Jacob's room. Her chest tightened as she stood in the doorway.

"It's okay, honey. Go right in. I'm sure he'll be glad to know you're here." The nurse gave Ann a gentle push before she walked away.

Ann stared down at her hero. His arms were completely bandaged along with one of his hands. His face, swollen with stitches above one eye. A tear escaped Ann and fell onto Jacob's cheek. She sniffed and gently wiped it with her finger.

His eyes fluttered open. "Hey, beautiful. I wondered when I'd see you again." His voice was hoarse. He tried to moisten his dry lips.

Ann retrieved some water from a table beside the bed and held it out for him. After he finished drinking, she collapsed in the chair at his side. She placed a hand on his shoulder, needing to touch him.

Jacob turned his head into her hand. His eyes were sleepy but he seemed determined to stay awake. "I remember you telling me something pretty important. I was hoping to hear it again." A familiar smirk lifted the corner of his mouth.

Ann leaned over and placed a kiss on Jacob's lips. "I told you, I love you. And, I meant every word."

Jacob's smile broadened as he held Ann's gaze. "I love you, Annie."

Chapter Twenty-Four

Jacob was home. Though he couldn't do much, at least he was with family. From his designated spot on the couch, he watched Ann busy herself with the household chores. She always hummed when she worked.

Even when making a mess.

He smiled. She told him she'd make home-made noodles for the chicken soup. The long, skinny noodles were now draped all over the kitchen to dry. He wasn't going to complain, he was sure it would be delicious, but he also never remembered his own mother making such a mess.

Ann turned around with her hands on her hips, looking for something. Jacob laughed.

"What?" she demanded.

"Come here, you've got flour all over your face."

Ann tried to wipe at it but her hands were too crusted with dough. She gave up, walked over to the couch and perched on the edge of the cushion. Jacob wiped her nose and forehead. "You're fun to watch."

Ann laughed but before she could respond Ethan walked in from his room. "Hey, what happened in there?" He gestured toward the kitchen. Jacob and Ann laughed some more as Ethan picked up the ointment for his dog. "Did we get to thank that vet who came and got Moses from the hospital?"

Ann shook her head. "He wasn't in when we picked him up. But I'll take you by later this week so you can personally thank him."

Ethan opened the door to step out. "Thanks, Ann."

Jacob shifted on the couch. "The kids love you, Annie."

"I love them, too." Their eyes met and exchanged a look of purpose. Before Jacob could add to it, his wounds drew Ann's gaze away. "How are you feeling? Do you need any pain medication?"

"Are you my nurse?"

Ann smiled. "I guess so."

"In that case, I think I need a sponge bath," Jacob teased her.

"You're a mess, Mr. Durham."

Jacob reached out with his good hand and drew Ann closer. "That's why I need you to stick around. I need some straightening out." His eyes shone brightly.

"I was so scared of losing you, of never seeing you again." Ann looked down at her hands and picked at the dried flour. "Of never being able to tell you," she brought her eyes to meet his, "how much you mean to me."

Jacob squeezed her hand. "Then marry me, and you'll have a lifetime to show me just how much."

Tears fell from Ann's eyes as she cupped Jacob's face in her dough encrusted hands. Her smile broadened as she leaned over to kiss him. "Yes. Oh yes!"

EPILOGUE

"As if the length of time before his proposal wasn't shocking enough, their engagement was. The following Sunday after Jacob Durham's stitches were removed, our local hero became husband to Ms. Annie McHaven, daughter of Mr. and Mrs. Gerald McHaven of Springfield, Ill. and niece of our local Mr. and Mrs. Sam Garrett. Congratulations to a beautiful couple."

Ann read the framed cutout from the local gazette. It was hard to imagine three years had already passed and she would soon deliver their second child.

Jacob walked up behind her, encircling Ann's swollen belly and whispered in her ear, "Are you ready, my beautiful bride?"

She leaned back into his embrace. "Definitely. I can't wait to hear Ethan and Emily's special. I'm so proud of how well they harmonize."

"You don't think Lucille plans to steal the show, do you?"

Ann laughed. "She better not. That's why we let Luke name her. If she misses announcing herself on his birthday, he'll be so disappointed."

Jacob gave her a gentle squeeze. "Then let's get going, Ethan's outside with Emily and Keaton. We'll stop by and get Grandpa and be on our way."

Ann could hear the pride in Jacob's voice. She felt it, too. Soon they would have the completed family they both dreamed about.

She folded her hand in her husband's large one and a love like no other surged through her. She turned and caught Jacob staring. A welcomed blush colored her cheeks as her eyes shone back.

". . . the coast in makes it all worth-while."

♡♡♡

A Note from the Author

I hope you enjoyed reading Abandoned Hearts as much as I enjoyed writing it. This story came about by a lot of different angles. A country road near our home inspired its start and the cougar elements stemmed from numerous sightings from the local community.

My family and I live in the area described in this book and in a home not too dissimilar from Jacob's cabin. We've had everything but a cougar in our yard and enjoy the excitement each new visitor brings. (As long as we're safely inside the house!)

Thank you for taking the time to read Jacob and Ann's story.

I enjoy hearing from my readers and can be found at http://www.reginatittel.blogspot.com, or you can leave me a message at reginatittel@gmail.com.

Also, if you enjoyed Abandoned Hearts, please consider leaving a review at amazon.com, barnesandnoble.com, or smashwords.com. Your encouraging words could be the catalyst someone else needs to purchase this book. Not only would you be sharing the Godly messages I shared with you, but you would also help promote me as an author.

Thanks again, and God bless!

Regina

Unexpected Kiss

The Ozark Durham Series Vol. 2

by

Regina Tittel

Halfway across the street, someone grabbed her elbow and pulled her to a stop. Carli turned. A pair of blue eyes captivated her. Like the sun dancing on top of rippled water, she became absorbed in their reflective light.

"Please, indulge me," a rugged voice drawled. The store-front stranger tipped her over his arm, while his other hand secured her waist. He leaned in close as her breath froze in expectation. With little time for thought or response, his lips sealed over hers with an electric current that burned straight to her heart.

All too soon, the man broke contact. Carli's breath hitched as she watched his eyes swirl with conflicting emotions. Before she could rationalize the moment, he drew her back to a stance and disappeared into the fading crowd.

A horn honked, followed by a hoot. Carli felt her cheeks redden and brought a trembling hand to her mouth. Her feet numbly moved her along the crosswalk. The scent of the stranger's spicy cologne clung in the air and rattled her senses. How could one single moment threaten to shatter her cleverly built façade?

♡♡♡

What does one kiss and Carli Williams have in common? Ethan Durham's heart.

What begins as an undercover photo shoot turns into a series of near death experiences geared toward the woman he loves. Why would someone want this heiress of an abandoned estate dead? Determined to keep her safe, Ethan not only has to give up his need for control, but he also must convince Carli of God's unconditional love so she can accept his.

Available Fall 2011

Coveted Bride

The Ozark Durham Series Vol. 3

by

Regina Tittel

"I'm sorry, Lindsey. I know this is hard. I don't understand why Mike chose to do things this way."

A few moments passed, she sniffed several times and wiped her eyes. "I could do this on my own. I don't have to remarry." She straightened. "This isn't the turn of the century. People don't do this anymore!"

Her ranting's wouldn't have made sense to just anyone, but Keaton knew exactly what she meant. Lindsey had allowed Mike to carry everything they owned in his name. Thus, giving him full control to do what he wished.

"You don't have to marry me if you don't want. You can find a way to work around this. He gave you a couple months, talk to a lawyer; see what your options are."

"Don't you mean *we* could talk to a lawyer to find a way out of this?"

"No." He looked her straight in the eye. "If you want out, you're on your own."

Lindsey's mouth dropped open. "What are you talking about? Look at what you're getting.

Keaton's gaze encircled the children and settled back on Lindsey. "I see a family. And the only woman I've ever wanted."

♡♡♡

Do arranged marriages still happen? For Lindsey Buchannan, yes. Everything was kept in her husband's name, giving him full control of all they owned. And upon his death-bed, he exposes his plan for his family's future. Lindsey has two months to marry Keaton Durham or a charity will inherit their trusts and home.

Determined to make it on her own, Lindsey rejects the idea immediately. But when a drug-addicted family member threatens her children for the sake of money, it is Keaton she continually turns to. Would it be so wrong to fall in love with the alluring man that sends shivers along her spine with just one look?

Available Spring 2012

Also Available
Amazon.com or Barnes & Noble.com
By Mildred Colvin

Learning to Lean - paperback $8.99
Kindle or Nook - $0.99
She has 3 kids and a daycare. He has 3 kids and is self- employed. They'd be better off as friends, right? Can they learn to lean on God?

Lesson of the Poinsettia - Kindle or Nook $0.99!
She lost her sight. He can't see God's leading when his daughter disobeys to visit the lady with the flowers. Can a little girl and a Poinsettia teach this couple to see with eyes of faith?

A New Life - paperback $8.99 Kindle or Nook - $0.99
She's City! He's Country! She just found out they have something in common. Her son!

Love Returned - paperback $8.99
Kindle or Nook - $0.99
She's in love. But his adopted son could be the baby she gave away nine years ago. If she confronts him, she'll lose his love, and he'll take her son away. If she keeps quiet and marries him, she'll have both husband and son, but be living a lie. Is there a happy ending?

Have **<u>The Ozark Durham Series</u>** sent to your home!

Item	Qty.	Price Ea.	Total
Abandoned Hearts (avail. now)		$ 11.95	
Unexpected Kiss (Fall 2010)		$ 11.95	
Coveted Bride (Spring 2011)		$ 11.95	
Merchandise Total			
$3.99 s/h			
MO Residents add 5.85% tax			
Order Total			

_____

Name   (Please Print)

_____

Address

_____

City   State   Zip

_____

Signature (if under 18, a parent or guardian must sign)

☐ Please contact me to discuss a discounted purchase for use in a youth group, book club, or other related service where five or more books are needed.

Make Check Payable to:

Regina Tittel

Rt. 1 Box 1795

Patton MO 63662

Made in the USA
Charleston, SC
09 November 2011